THE COLOR OF BLOOD

by

Mona Kabbani

MONA KABBANI

ISBN-13: 9798874358617

First Edition, February 2024

Edited by Spencer Hamilton

www.spencerhamiltonbooks.com

www.nerdywordsmith.com

Cover Illustration by Mona Kabbani

Instagram @moralityinhorror

I offered the snake a pomegranate
it found the tiny seeds amusing
the color vibrant
the flesh soft.

The snake thanked me
but found it could not tell the difference
and when it bit my throat
i understood love.

To knowing when it's venom.

Content Warning: The following contains graphic scenes of sex and violence intended for a mature audience.

THE COLOR OF BLOOD

by

Mona Kabbani

MONA KABBANI

POLYCHROMATIC

MONA KABBANI

It has not rained for some time, yet the city brims with rainbows. Colors that pulse like heartbeats.

Up ahead, a young boy trails behind his mother, one hand gripping the back of her skirt, the other wrapped around the vanilla ice cream cone he holds high into the sky. When that cone is inevitably scooped away by a seagull who only knows the color of survival, the young boy's hue will morph from its current untainted yellow to some horrid combination of colors, like scarlet and dark blue. No, not purple. In this circumstance, not possibly something so beautiful.

None but I can perceive such hues.

None as far as I know.

I hope to witness this corruption firsthand. To see that young boy drain of excitement and fill with a mixture of frustration and sorrow. But his mother, surrounded by the color of loyalty, stops, turns to face him, and corrects his posture. She guides his grip so that both hands hold the cone in front of his chest, where he can easily consume his ice cream and keep it away from the birds.

The boy smiles. His color remains only yellow.

I scan the rest of the boardwalk. If I look up at the Ferris wheel, as I often do, I can see a ring of multicolored light, an aura that changes with each rotation: the color of anticipation where it rises, fear at its peak, and relief on the way down. Sometimes I see other colors. Most commonly romance or sexual tension. When bodies nod off on their second or third rotation, they strobe. The same principle applies to the rollercoasters, the flyers, or whatever else might fling bodies this way and that.

It's why I love the boardwalk so much.

I stick my hand into the pouch at my side, pull out a few pencils, and press them to the sketchpad on my lap. This is both my release and my curse. A release because what better expression of oneself is there than art? A curse because the colored pencils never get it right. There is an entire spectrum lost on their pigment. They'll never be vibrant enough, never expressive enough, to reveal what I see.

Still, I try. To most, I succeed.

When the girl steps too close to the bench where I sit and knocks the pad from my hands, I don't lash out as she removes her earbuds to apologize.

"Oh, jeez, hon," she says. "I am so, *so* sorry!"

I bend over to pick up the fallen items, as does she, and our fingers touch atop my work in progress. A phoenix, which is so rudimentary, so juvenile, except for the fact that my phoenix bleeds rainbows as it was meant to, rising from a nostalgic playground. The girl hesitates, as do I, and we lift our chins to look at each other. We're quite close, I realize. About three inches apart.

"That's a beautiful drawing," she compliments.

"Thank you." I'm smiling. And I'm flattered. Really. Because, to be quite frank, I hate this piece.

"Are you some kind of artist?"

"You might say that."

Her nose scrunches with a blush as she registers the color of my eyes—contact lenses, to hide what lies beneath. Today they are slate blue with a subtle hint of violet. "Regal and mysterious" is the look I'm going for. Contrasted against my dark hair, bangs that fall just across the right side of my face, some might say I'm impossible to resist.

"Are you . . ." the girl begins. "Are you, uh, famous or something?"

I chuckle. I have no doubt she'd know my work if she saw it. She just can't recognize me.

"Some might say."

I registered her color prior to this incident. I'd seen it in my periphery before she collided with me. But seeing it up close now, it's breathtaking. A shade of blue I rarely see. So light and airy, as if coy. Like merely perceiving it could cause it to slip away. It makes the blue of her eyes so dull in comparison.

I assess the situation. She's in runner's clothes and, considering the way she seems to be flirting with me, I assume there is no significant other around for me to worry about. Nor do I see any friend on the sideline, tapping their foot with wild impatience.

There are no devices on her wrists. Only her phone, tucked away in the inner pocket of her cycling shorts. That's easy enough. When I ask her if she wants my number, I'll take her phone and make sure all location data is turned off. If that doesn't work, I'll simply vanish. It would be a shame, but no color is worth the risk.

"Were you planning to enjoy the rest of your day alone?" I ask.

Her eyes widen, mouth moving around words she is unable to speak. Her hand retracts slightly, and I fear I've made a miscalculation. But then she sticks her fingers through the loops that bind my sketchpad and stands to hand the item back to me with a smile. She pulls out her phone—the one I will soon enough wipe—clicks the pause button on her music, and looks to the sky, squinting against the sun.

"I'd just begun my run," she comments. "But I suppose I've been good this week. I can substitute it with a nice stroll if you're interested?"

I suck in a deep gulp of air—the deepest breath I have taken all day—hoping to inhale some of her color, but all I get is the scent of sunscreen and lavender. I lean over to place the pencils and sketchpad in the pouch at my side, stand, and readjust the strap around my shoulder. When she registers my full height, the curve of my muscles and stomach through my tight, long-sleeve shirt, how my hips taper, and how my paint-stained jeans are held up by a thick backside and muscular thighs, her color brightens and she gulps.

I've got her.

"What's your name?" I ask.

"Caroline. What's yours?"

The name I tell her does not matter. It is not real, of course.

Still, she repeats it—"Nicholas?"—rolling the false identity around her tongue like a cold marble. "I like the sound of that."

I grin and ask, "As a jogger, have you ever been to the far end of the boardwalk?"

"No," she says, her curiosity piqued. "Why?"

"Oh, there's a beautiful spot you must see."

We start our walk. The spot I've told her about is real—and far away from any CCTV cameras. It overlooks a bluff where waves that are just so dull in color to me crash and thunder. The view takes other people's breath away, as I'm sure it will hers.

Should that happen, the rest will be like clockwork.

I take one final glance at the Ferris wheel: those colors, those auras of passenger souls I could watch all day spiraling around and around.

"Oh!" I exclaim, stopping in my tracks.

The girl turns to me with sudden concern, her eyebrows knitting together, bottom lip pouting, color dimming.

With a disarming smile, I reach out with my empty, open

hand, and say, "How rude of me. Before we begin our date, would you like my phone number?"

~

I am, in fact, a professional artist. A painter, to be precise. I am quite good at it and have made a fine fortune for myself from my work. Enough to own a penthouse in one of this city's finest buildings, as well as its rooftop, where I have built a nifty little incinerator. My inspiration comes from my unique comprehension of the world, my ability to perceive what I have coined as the *divine spectrum*, something no one else can see but all can feel when gazing upon my paintings. Critics revel in my genius, calling my collections emotional masterpieces, quintessential imagery for the generation that cannot speak, and me the "modern king of color." For this, I lack idols. But if someone were to hold a gun to my head and demand I answer the most asked question in the creative world—*Who inspires you?*—I would say the man who brought "action painting" to fame.

Not for his art, per se, but for his mind.

By 1947, the American artist, Jackson Pollock, father to the drip technique, stopped naming his paintings entirely. Instead, he numbered them. He did not want evocative titles to take away from the experience. To unknowingly prompt viewers to search for what isn't there or to deter them from creating connections on their own.

I do not paint in his abstract style—my creations are much more realized than his—but I do find romanticism in his choice. A play with the unknown. An invitation for viewers to dare gaze upon something with no guardrails. To potentially fall, to spiral down a maelstrom of possibilities, none of which might be correct, all of which might be true.

I like that he, so self-assured in his art, did not fear his viewers missing the point.

I like that he didn't give a fuck what anyone believed they did or didn't see.

~

She is soaking wet, and I do not enjoy the sensation of her fingertips on my waist. If my hands weren't around her throat, my mouth not kissing her sweaty, euphoric expression, I might have grabbed her wrists and pinned them above her head. Just to get her to stop touching me. But she likes it like this. I can tell because she is strobing beneath me. The effect is amazing, that coy blue flashing in and out, intermingling with lust and an accent of apprehension. I find it interesting that her color never strays too far from this natural palette, all shades a variant, as if there isn't much depth to her beyond this.

That's fine. Not much of a fireworks show, but one I enjoy all the same.

Her tongue punches out from between her lips, and I suck on the muscle despite my desire to return the saliva back into her mouth via gagging. I suck and kiss and think about that wavelength of light, that brilliant dance. How I've rewired my disgust toward bodies to become pleasure for the sake of the spectacle. But still, it would be nice if she weren't so . . . wet.

I let go of her neck, and she gasps for air. The color returns to her face as she shudders and clenches around me. I reach down and rub her clit, gradually speeding up my movements. She screams and her color flares. Her pulse quickens, like pistons on an accelerating train, until her screams reach a pitch I can hardly bear, and a single burst of color lights up the room like a flash grenade.

I wince at its radiance. She can't see it, but I can. That dazzling light I will pluck from the metaphorical sky to place in my pocket and create worlds with.

As she experiences her comedown, I remove myself from her and lie on my side. I ask Carly or Carol—I can't seem to remember her name now, so I will call her Number Ten—if she would like to go for another round. She wheezes, her chest rising and falling as she grips the tarp beneath us, points to her chest, and shakes her head no.

I thought runners were supposed to have efficient lungs. This, I do not say to her.

When her breath steadies, she takes in my studio, the nearly 3,000 square feet dedicated to my art. I think this sight—the abused canvases, limbless sculptures, supplies organized like a personal art shop, all atop a massive, stained vinyl tarp—is what got her to make that final leap. To share her body with me.

"You know," she starts, "I used to paint a lot when I was younger."

I place my hand on the small of her stomach, trace my finger around her belly button, and offer a warm smile.

"Tell me about it," I say.

She shrugs. "There's not much to tell. My parents divorced when I was a freshman in high school. I'm an only child, so it was hard. My therapist suggested I take on a hobby. Something creative. So I picked up a paintbrush."

"What did you paint?"

Her cheeks burn a rosy pink and her lips tighten into a thin line like she's embarrassed to say.

"Go on," I encourage.

"Well, nothing as amazing as all this, but . . ."

Another moment of hesitation. I tuck a lock of hair behind her ear and brush her lips like I can marionette her into speaking.

"I'd paint myself on different animals," she admits. "Like lions and tigers. My favorite was one of me riding a dolphin into the deep sea. I guess it made me feel strong or like I had other options. Like I could escape and become a part of another family. A more put-together herd than my own."

My smile grows. "That's adorable."

She rolls her eyes with a laugh. "I know. Kind of pathetic, huh?"

"I don't think so. Not at all."

"Well, I haven't painted in years, so . . ."

She looks at me and I look at her, understanding passing between us. I think to bring myself to kiss her again, but she gets up, peeling her wet skin from the ground. She wraps a corner of the vinyl tarp around her nakedness, only to reveal more tarp beneath, but this she does not notice. Her feet press forward—heel to toe, heel to toe—and I watch her approach one of my canvases propped up on an easel.

"You really like phoenixes, don't you?" she asks.

"Not particularly," I respond. "They're a new subject I'm testing out. I'm not sure how I feel about them yet."

She reaches as if to touch the unfinished, still-wet paint, then stops herself. Not that I would mind. She'll add leagues to this piece soon enough.

I stand and approach her, wrap my arms around her shoulders, and pull her in. She melts into me, finding the gesture romantic, but really I'm eyeing the canvas, debating what's missing, what's needed.

"For me, painting is like a spiritual awakening," I say. "It's different from sculpting. When I sculpt, I'm building something wholly separate. But when I paint, I'm seeing into myself. I'm seeing myself through shapes and colors. That's the goal, at least. It never quite works out that way, and I wonder if that's the point. If the torture of never being able to truly know, to accurately express oneself, drives one to create."

She nods, thinks on this, and finally says, "A tortured artist." She says it with a touch of awe, and I find myself disappointed that this is all she can manage. "I see."

I know she doesn't. Not truly. It's impossible for her to see.

She grazes the underside of my jaw. She is thinking of all the ways she can help me. Fix my soul like her therapist fixed hers whilst keeping me damaged enough to still be a success.

But she doesn't know. And I can't fault her for the ignorance, can I?

A soul needs to exist first in order to be fixed.

I lean us both over and grab the bone-white palette knife encased in a soft orange glow from the easel ledge. I hold it before us, running my callused thumb over the blade. I take her hand and curl her palm around the handle. I carved this handle myself into intricate ribs that hit like acupressure points when pressed just right. She moans in pleasure as I constrict her grip for her. I'm around her like a petal-veined snake, hypnotizing her, sheathing her in decadence.

"I could paint you, if you'd like," I whisper into her ear, sliding one tantalizing hand down the small of her belly. "I could paint you riding that phoenix all the way into the sunset."

Her warm breath heightens as I bring the palette knife to her chest, tracing the rise and fall of her collarbones.

"I'd like that," she says.

"Good."

So with her assent, I run the edge of the knife across her throat, splitting the skin, the muscles, the cartilage. Color bursts forth in a grand arc, and it's magnificent. Like parting space and time and creating heaven's gates with one fell swoop. The arc weakens into a trickle as the heart continues to pump blood to a brain that will take another moment or two to die. It must have been shocking for her, given that palette knives are not meant to be so sharp, but as I've noted, I carved this one myself.

There is a gurgle, a *pop* from her throat as she drowns in her own blood, and I would reassure her in her dying moments that she will be immortalized forever, that viewers will come from far and wide just to catch a glimpse of her, but I am tired now and she is already dead.

I let go and her body falls to the floor, color pooling on the tarp around her. I'm staring at the canvas and now it is my turn to be in awe.

I was right: that color, that ethereal blue, is what was missing. And it did not vanish like the coy pigment it was after being perceived. In fact, quite the opposite. It's thriving under my sight. It's *glowing*.

Between the fresh streaks, the phoenix rises, hovering above all, wings spread in glorious dominance, and I think to myself this subject has a lot more in store for me than I initially thought.

~

Jackson Pollock knocked down a wall to create his famous *Mural* (1943) for the Guggenheim. He was given a canvas twenty feet wide by eight feet tall and told to paint whatever he desired. His contract came with a stipend hefty enough to allow him to quit his job as a janitor and pursue the profession of art full-time. Receiving the opportunity, he destroyed a part of his apartment to fit the enormity of his future.

Although I am already leagues ahead of Pollock's timeline, I like to think that is what I am doing as I drive the sole of my boot into the chest cavity of Number Ten. Her sternum makes a satisfying *crunch*, and I drool at all I'll do with those bits of bone. Perhaps make a collage or use them as scales on a sculpture. I've already detached and skinned her limbs with the bone saws I store atop the blades of my ceiling fan. The limbs dangle over a bucket to collect what color is left in their veins. The midsection is not something I particularly enjoy dealing with, besides the occasional intestine play (with gloves on, of course). And who can blame me? They look like glowworms crawling within a nest of bioluminescent flesh.

Remarkable.

I pull my foot out with little resistance besides a nick from one protruding rib I've damaged. I've probably burst the heart and lungs by now, but that's no matter. I haven't been in the mood to use flesh for a medium as of late, and her lungs are a dull color, a diseased color. Asthma, most likely. It would explain the difficulty breathing.

I kneel and dig my fingers beneath the flap of skin that leads up to Number Ten's right breast. She wasn't well endowed, which I prefer. It makes peeling back this part much easier. Like Velcro with a touch greater resistance. Beneath is the surface of her ribcage. It's riddled with muscle fibers and sinew. I'll gut her and strip as much as I can, then stick this along with the limbs and head in the tub of water on my roof. It's private, so no one goes up there besides me, and this city stinks enough to excuse the smell this process makes. Once the flesh is all soft and jellylike, I'll scrub down the bones, then use hydrogen peroxide to achieve the purity I need. This will allow that color to shine through all the brighter from the marrow. Whatever remains I'll drain and burn to ash.

All those dazzling bones will go to good use; experimental sculptures, textured landscapes, another palette knife.

Discarded to the side is Number Ten's head. Her mouth gapes, dull eyes wide—an expression overall unbecoming. I place two fingers on her lids, shut them, then do the same to her jaw, only for it to fall open again. I'll have to be careful. I don't want to damage a perfectly good jaw. My fingers run up her cheekbones, over her eyebrows. They thread through her hair so I can get a grip and lift her head as I stand tall. I raise my fist so her face is level with my own.

I realize that in this moment I probably look absurd to the human eye. Naked except for steel-toed combat boots, levitating a head like it's a holy weapon.

What a groundbreaking painting I would be.

I rotate the head so its dull expression looks to the heavens and tuck the thing in the nook of my arm. I walk to an easel, stare at the canvas, and pick up a paintbrush from the ledge. I stick the brush handle between my teeth, then search my shelves.

Blue. I need blue.

I grab a tube of oil paint which my keen eye discerns most closely matches the blue emitting from this body. With a careless squeeze, I pour a spiral onto the bloody stump of a neck, which I've readjusted under my arm to be used as my palette. The string of paint loops around the severed brain stem like a coil. I toss the tube back onto the shelf where it clatters against vials of color and return to my canvas.

Number Ten asked me if I like phoenixes, and I told her the truth. I'm not quite sure yet. They're an idea I'm toying with for the next gallery exhibition. On this canvas, a phoenix is crawling out of a black pit rather than resurrecting from its ashes. There are many things this could symbolize, stories it could tell that I've only just begun to uncover, but what I do know is this painting will make its viewers feel something even if they do not fully comprehend what that feeling is.

It just needs that extra touch.

I take the paintbrush from my lips, dip the bristles into the folds of bleeding flesh until Number Ten's color coats them, then dip into the paint, swirling the two around until they are blended.

With care and much concentration, my bottom lip sucked between my teeth, I paint.

It only takes a few brush strokes to see the difference. A dot around the eyes, a slash to accentuate the feathers. It's like the painting comes to life. As though the phoenix is crawling toward you, determined to reach you. A blazing storm of red and blue fire. All the elements to send chills down one's spine.

I see it as a glowing effect, an aura unmatched. I'm not sure what my audience sees. Not a simple painting, and surely not the blood of a young girl who has just been brutally slaughtered and turned into the greatest medium known to man. But I know they see art. They see a depiction beyond all human understanding. They feel it in their souls.

The painting isn't quite done yet. I still have months until the gallery owner requires my new collection. I'll probably revisit this painting once or twice more as I walk across my studio and catch it in the corner of my eye. But for now, it is near perfect.

On the bottom righthand corner of the canvas, I sign my name with the same blue color.

Void.

That's it. No more, no less.

I drop the paintbrush, bristle end first, into a cup of cloudy water, then release Number Ten's head. It falls to the floor with a dull *thud*. The layers of vinyl tarp help to mute out any harsh sounds. They also help as an easy-to-assemble garbage bag once I'm done and ready to clean up the evidence.

Poof! Gore, be gone!

Until then I have much cleaning to do. Whatever I do not wish to keep will need to be gathered and thrown into the incinerator. But not now. Now, I want to soak this all in.

I turn around, stretch my arms out, fists clenched, muscles flexed, lungs filled, and roar from the force. It feels good to make progress. I feel like a god.

A pain blooms in my eye. I hiss and curl over, finger hovering right in front of the perpetrating socket. There's paint and blood all over my hands. It would be a poor choice to stick those into my contacts.

I hurry to the bathroom. I run my hands under warm water until all the blue is washed from them, then look at myself in the mirror. What looks back is a man who appears normal, not a color about him. Just a chiseled face, a nose, a mouth, lips, teeth, dark eyebrows that are tattooed on. With one finger, I tug on my bottom lid. With my thumb and index finger, I pinch the contact and remove it from my cornea.

What's left is a pupil. No iris. Solely a dark pupil swimming in a milky expanse, a black hole that dilates until it's adjusted to the light and pain. It's quite disturbing to look at, even for me, and I've always found it funny how, although I can see a spectrum of color unattainable to others, all sense of color is bleached from my own person.

I remove the other contact and place them both in their lens case on the shelving above the sink. I run my fingers—with pads so smooth they do not leave evidence of my existence—through my hair, pull until the glue comes loose from my bald scalp, and stick the wig on the rack behind the mirror. I lower my head and splash water on my face, removing whatever rouge I've placed in strategic positions to make me look more alive. Like blood flows properly through my veins. Like I'm warm.

I return to the mirror. There is no color about me, no gorgeous aura that surrounds me like a halo. At least not from what I can see in my reflection. My eyes can't perceive color when it is captured or reflected, not in photographs nor mirrors nor windows nor bodies of water, and I've made myself bleed enough to know that none exists for me in the first place.

I am a blank canvas. A nothing person.

A void that can be decorated and designed but never filled.

~

I have been asked to come into the gallery today for a special request. Typically I'd refuse, but the owner pleaded so pathetically I had to oblige. I like her enough, although I wish I could say she's done more for me than any agent ever would. A benevolent woman? No. She's greedy for the fat stacks of cash shoved into her pocket, the gallery's increasing fame, the applauded success after each exclusive exhibition. What I like is that I know this about her. I know what drives her. And I'll do her this favor. It's always important to keep a few good deeds in one's back pocket.

Besides, I needed to get out of my studio. It stinks.

A local university has sent their art majors to learn firsthand about the intricacies of creation and curation. Twelve of the greatest minds their educational program has to offer stand before me now, wide-eyed and slack-jawed. Colors pooling together like a rainbow of sewage.

If I had hair, I'd be tearing it out in clumps right now. But Void doesn't have hair—in this persona, my main one, I am bald with brown eyes—and even if I were wearing a wig, it wouldn't achieve the same effect. The same root-ripping compensatory pain.

I keep calm. I don't lash out even when the girl at the front of the group asks me, "Mr. Void, what paint did you use for your *Architecture of the Nuclear* piece over there?"

I bite the inside of my cheek. I make myself bleed.

"Watercolor," I say through a tight smile.

"It looks bumpy in some parts."

I nod. "Good observation." A lie. It's not. Any novice could point out a watercolor collage when they see one. "It does, in fact, have texture to it. I wanted to add a depth of field while also maintaining the purity of the medium. So I molded some papier-mâché into the shapes I desired and let the watercolor soak for a seamless blend."

Not papier-mâché. Bones. The stapes from a human ear.

"It's important to explore every medium," I continue. "To work every tool of creation between your hands so not only can your mind memorize its consistency, but your body can understand its nature."

The girl's eyes glaze over. I wish I could scream.

Hands raise, popping from the crowd like moles.

"Mr. Void, what's your most *favorite* medium?"

"Mr. Void, what's your most *favorite* piece?"

"Mr. Void, what's your most *favorite* inspiration?"

"Do you prefer to paint in the morning or at night?"

That last question actually isn't so bad. At least we're getting somewhere away from the asinine inquiries a kindergartener might make. I thought these were prestigious art majors. I thought they would be beyond all this.

My mouth moves, but at this point my mind discovers it's safe to detach. I can answer these questions on autopilot. Instead, I think about this color palette before me. If I could turn something so dull into a revelation.

It would be a challenge. One I would want to take on? Perhaps not.

"I prefer oil paint. My sculptures are not on display, but clay is a joy to work with.

"I can't answer that question. They're all my favorite.

"Jackson Pollock. And also, life.

"Well, let's see, lighting can really affect a painting's—"

I stop. Something out the front windows catches the corner of my eye. Something that moves quickly, but not so fast as to escape my senses. Like it wants to be seen. Like it wants to be chased.

"If you'll all please excuse me for just one moment."

I'm out the door before anyone can protest. I barely notice the hike in temperature from frigid air-conditioning to boiling asphalt. All I'm focused on is color. I see color all around, from people idling about to glows emanating from within occupied cars, but nothing like what I just saw. Not the subject I want. Not the subject I'm pursuing.

And I *know* I saw it.

I face down the street. Just as I do, I see it turn a corner, its tail end barely visible, simply a wisp, a smokey finger curling for me to come closer before it disappears.

I hustle, but I hold back a full sprint. It would be a comical sight—the famed Void in a suit and tie going over eight miles per hour down a city sidewalk. What is he chasing? Why does he look so desperate? No, I'll keep it to a hurried walk, but on the inside I'm on fire, my soul panicked with urgency.

I skid around the corner, the rubber of my soles barely maintaining contact with the concrete. I stop.

There she is.

And here I am, a blessed witness.

She stands before a store's window display. Her index finger hovers in front of the pane of glass, moving here and there as her lips work around a discussion she is having with herself. She is tall, perhaps my height, and her skin is a deep olive, stark against her white chemise.

Stark against so much more. Against—my *god*, that *color*.

My knees grow weak. They could wobble and I could fall beneath the weight of what's before me. But they don't. I won't let them. I need to maintain my composure.

I need to devour every moment of this.

Her color is like nothing I have ever seen. It's dark—so dark it's nearly black, but not quite; just a thin degree off, a hair's breadth so thin that *Cyclamen* petals would weep at its delicacy. Depending on its angle, depending on how the shadows and sunlight move about this way and that, it shifts. Like an oil slick. Like it's bored with being perceived one way for too long. It pulses around her like the corona of a supernova. Like something that could wipe out entire civilizations with a single burst. An angel come to deliver its reckoning.

When she turns to continue her way down the street, I follow, dumbly, as though her color has a mass whose gravity pulls only me. She stops at other stores, glancing into their windows. She looks at street signs and makes another turn or two. I find it interesting that her color doesn't change with her reactions like it does for most. When she gapes in wonder or bounces with excitement or furrows her brow in confusion, her color does not follow. It shifts when it pleases. Almost as if it has a mind of its own.

She pulls out a map, squints at the lines, then looks up at the street sign. She's clearly not from here, a tourist perhaps. This could be my only chance to approach her. To get closer to that color, to loom over her until I can touch it. Until it envelops me.

I take a step toward her.

I'll ask if she needs my help.

I take another step.

I'll point out that she looks lost.

A light breeze brushes a lock of brown hair from her slender shoulder. Her heels dig into the sidewalk, and she rotates away from me. She's facing an alleyway. A lone, dark alleyway. A shortcut to the other side of this avenue. She steps inside and I peer around the corner after her.

The alleyway is long, poorly lit, and windowless. I reach under my suit jacket into my back pocket. My fingers wrap around the handle, and I pull out a palette knife like the one I keep in my studio only smaller. One I keep on me for good luck.

I readjust the knife in my grip and place myself before the entrance of the alleyway. My blood is audibly pumping in my ears, my heart booming, and for a moment I wonder if she can hear my excitement. My muscles trembling, my breath shallow and hungry. She's not too far yet, walking slowly, very slowly. It's tantalizing. Like she wants me. Like that color is whispering, *Come hither . . .* , its pigment making the shadows that lie here look like mere scuff marks on dilapidated concrete.

There are people all around. Right behind me, meters in front of her. They would see. Of course they would see. I've been spotted in this area. I just ran from a lecture to be here, for god's sake.

I curse myself and finalize my resolve, regretfully sheathing my palette knife. I refuse to blink, my eyes wide to absorb this moment in all its capacity. I pray it stains my bones, infiltrates so deep I could never possibly forget the hue.

I stand at the entrance of the alleyway, unable to pursue her. Unable to act. I wish I could tell her all the ways her mere existence destroys and rebuilds every cell of my being. The foundation I've erected my life upon. How she sets my soul on fire.

But no color is worth the risk. Not even this one.

~

I can't stop thinking about her.

When I walk through my studio door, the sight of all that I have created sickens me. I've not created *art*; I've created a hollow shell, an empty cavern I fill with meaningless ideas and worthless notions. None of it is real art. Not when a color like that exists out there, just casually strolling about the city streets.

I can't stop fixating on her. I simply *can't*. There was the truth of the world, hidden all this time, laughing at me as it watched me create. Laughing as I claimed to know things I do not.

I know nothing.

I feel sick.

I trudge into the center of my studio, the ceiling fan's light like a spotlight so that rotten tomatoes can be thrown at my face and I can do nothing but accept my fate. I stare at the partially mulched body at my feet, the buckets of that girl's blue color now so disappointing to me. My sculptures . . . my canvases.

It smells like shit. It *looks* like shit.

I can't bear the sight of it any longer.

I pick up the corners of the tarp and bring them together to be tied off. I haul this makeshift sack to the front of my studio, where its mocking glow is out of my line of sight. The buckets of blood I pour down the kitchen drain. By now my disappointment has ignited into rage and self-hatred, and suddenly it is not enough to dispose of the body but to dispose of my work. To self-flagellate with the destruction of my art.

I tour my studio, tearing down canvases, kicking in sculptures. Porcelain and shredded linen arc through the stale air in the wake of my rage. My fingers dig deep into mounds of clay, wishing I could conjure fire to my fingertips in the hopes of melting it all into a vat of bubbling garbage. I grab tubes of paint and squeeze their contents down my toilet. *Flush.* Grab more and squeeze them into my bathroom sink. Acrylic paint and resin fly out my studio windows. Damn the street below. I hope the pigeons have their fill and fall over dead.

I pry off a femur from an unfinished sculpture and hold it over my head like a club, about to bring it down upon my central work in progress—the phoenix climbing out of the hole.

I stop.

The phoenix stares at me and I stare back. Despite the effort, its talons just grasping the hole's exit, its wings tensed with the strain of pulling itself forward when it is meant to fly, its expression is cool. Calm and collected.

It will come to you, its expression says. *It knows it will reach you.*

And here I am, an ape holding a crusty bone over my head, as though this will cure my problems. As though destruction isn't a primitive man's game.

Suddenly I hate myself in a new light.

I drop the femur. It clatters to the layers of vinyl tarp below, dull yet clunky, and my brain rattles with it.

How silly of me. I am looking at this all wrong, through the wrong lens. This encounter was not a loss. It was not a taunting of my artistic failure nor a carrot on the end of a stick I'll never reach. It was not the world showing me what exists that I may never have. No, not at all. It was quite the opposite.

It was discovery.

The earth moves in revolutions, slowly yet assuredly. All it takes is time and patience. If something of this nature exists in a world where only I can perceive it, it belongs to me. Surely she will come to me.

She must.

She is owed to me.

~

I stay up all night thinking about her. Thinking about her smooth skin—not a bump, not a callus—and how her color caresses her body in all the right places. How it lives on her, morphs to her every movement, a soul materialized, a doppelgänger in new form. Truly nothing else could ever belong so perfectly. Like taking the beak off a duck, ripping the wings and flippers away, and trying to convince people it is still a duck. That it is not something dead and broken.

She is an angel incarnate, and without her color, she would not be her.

I wonder about that color. I try to imagine it in my mind's eye, to hold its image so I can wonder at it some more, but it flutters away. So I must think, instead, of its *concept*. I wonder how, in the divine spectrum of all that I can see, this color managed to slip into reality. To emerge within my realm of understanding, pop up from somewhere between the shades and say, *Hello! Did you not see me here?*

I wonder what it would be like to break her skin. What would come pouring out? If only I could see her in my memory for a moment longer instead of being teased so painfully. I could then better imagine her inverted, bleeding that color. I could imagine her bones alight with it.

Blood rushes. I feel myself stiffen. Heat rises to my cheeks. With unease, I place my hands on my crotch. This is unusual. I push down as though I can push the very instinct away from me. It only grows. This has never happened before. It swells and it swells and suddenly I feel heavy. So very heavy. I want to scream. I want to tear open my ceiling and demand relief, demand that my chest stop constricting and my jaw stop tensing to the point of breakage. I'd weep, but instead I think of her. I think of her finger against the store window. I think of how easily her expression showed her delight, an open book unafraid of the world looking in. I think of how I remember all these details of her, yet I can barely remember her color.

I wonder if she would be insulted. I don't think she would. I think she would be kind.

I calm down. I think of her smile as I hold my aching erection. I think of her walk and the way she searched the space around her like she could pluck answers to philosophical questions from city corners.

I think of her with feathered wings ascending into the sky toward me.

I think of her as I eventually find relief.

~

My phone vibrates.

I ignore it.

It vibrates again—and then again and again and again until I am certain I am losing it.

I sit up in bed, reach for the phone on my nightstand, and read the screen.

Seven missed calls, all from the gallery owner. An eighth incoming call startles me and I answer, placing the cool glass against my ear.

"Are you fucking kidding me, Void?" she hisses.

"Good morning to you, too," I reply, my eye twitching at her high-pitched admonishment.

"Explain yourself."

"Explain what?"

An incredulous guffaw. "Now you're playing stupid? You abandoned the lecture not fifteen minutes in. That relationship is ruined now, do you understand? *Ruined.*"

"I had an emergency."

"I hope it was worth it."

I think on this before replying, "It was."

There's a pause, a silence I know the gallery owner wants me to fill with apologies and promises. What I'd like to tell her is that the entire thing was a misuse of time and that I'd be invoicing her for my services rendered yet wasted. I decide against it.

"Send the university an email on my behalf," I offer. "Apologize for the interruption—"

"Abandoning a lecture is a *cancellation*, Void."

"Fine. The cancellation. Make it out like I'm on my knees begging for forgiveness if it pleases you. And then give their entire art department a free pass to the gallery."

Another pause, but this time I know she's weighing efficacy, deciding if she can get any more out of me.

"Will you do another lecture for them?" she asks.

I bite my tongue and reply, "Maybe."

"Fine."

She hangs up. That's not good. I sigh.

I'll stop by the art gallery. I'll make my heartfelt apologies in person and enjoy seeing the owner's navy blue color melt. She'll apologize in turn for what I know she will come to realize was an embarrassing misuse of my precious time. I'll smile. She'll smile. We'll make up as we laugh with little inflection.

But first things first. I deep clean my studio. Rubber gloves, microfiber cloths, baking soda, distilled white vinegar, liquid dish soap, hydrogen peroxide. Therapy. Meditation. Like scrubbing away the dirt and dust that coats my very insides, weighing me down, allowing me freedom for what's to come. The smells are divine. Cleanliness and all that.

I have entirely forgotten what Number Ten looks like. She is safely and securely sealed away in a tarp along with so many discarded art supplies. I cannot tell where she starts and where my own art begins.

She might consider that a compliment. If she were still alive.

I throw the sack over my back. It squelches once as it hits my spine, the contents compressing. I take the flight of stairs just outside my studio door and use my keys to unlock the roof. There, I toss the sack into the industrial incinerator I had built—under the table, of course, all cash. *I'm a paranoid artist,* I told the consultant. *I don't want a single soul laying eyes upon the art I decide to throw away.* "Art" being subjective. The consultant took my words at face value, signed the papers, and had this wonderful furnace built. It even has *VOID* engraved in an elegant script just beneath the switch. I seal the door shut, lock it, flip the switch. The process begins.

So fucking simple. I love it when things are simple.

As Number Ten burns I take in the city skyline with a deep inhale. The sky looks like mango sorbet and excitement this early morning. Birds fly about. Smoke the color of that coy blue rises from the incinerator's exhaust pipe and shields the sun's rays from reaching me. It's too bad my neighbors only see gray clouds and the smell of what they've been told is acrylic and canvas on fire. For a cremation, this sight is quite beautiful.

Jackson Pollock did not have the funds to return home and attend his father's funeral when he died in 1933. I wonder who would have attended Number Ten's funeral. I wonder if they would appreciate the service I've given her.

I take another moment of silence, speculation, and appreciation. I bow my head to the city and return to my apartment knowing that if I opened my incinerator now, it would be empty except for a thin pile of colorless dust.

~

I take a cab to the gallery and pay in cash.

When I enter, I am immediately greeted by the owner. Despite her age, her hearing is like an elephant's; I swear she could sniff me out in a crowded room. She wears a red, shin-length Abigail with lantern sleeves and a matching ribbon to cinch at her thin waist. Her lipstick is meant to match her dress but is a few shades too light. She, nor anyone else for that matter, would know unless I told them. Although she deals in art every waking day, she does not have the eyes I have. She does not have my sight.

Her arms are held out wide, face filled with unabashed delight. I allow her to embrace me.

She apologizes. Of course she apologizes—she is a smart woman who can see the bigger picture, who understands that time is a fragile, finite thing and what a waste to give it to those who cannot tell oil from gouache.

With her hands on my shoulders, she holds me at arm's length. Our hips still touch, and for a moment I wonder if she will lean in to kiss me.

Instead she says, "While you're here, shall we talk about the next collection?"

I grin. "I'd love to."

"I'm thinking this season we introduce something fresh into the mix. Perhaps a massive sculpture?" She winks.

Now my smile is genuine. I am content with this news.

"That would be exquisite. I think you'll be more than pleased with how I'm choosing to portray my new subject."

A phone rings in the distance. The owner's eyes perk, and she twirls toward the sound. Honeysuckle from her perfume smacks me square across the face and I reel back, hiding my disgust.

"Oh, you'll have to excuse me," she says. "Let's speak in about fifteen minutes."

She hurries away and I am left in front of my collection, which I have seen more times than any artist should. Viewing one's own work is an invitation for harsh self-criticism that amounts to nothing but pain. Still, I would rather paint in monotone than feign interest in anyone else's work, and the colors walking around in here are all so drab.

I turn to my collection. This season I focused on the mundane, painted in high vibrancy with colors and shading so meticulously plotted the onlooker will struggle at first to distinguish the normal, everyday items from the bigger design. The sight as their eyes grow wide after minutes of speculation, when they finally realize the image is an angled frame of a whisk or a spice rack, never fails to satisfy me. The green that outlines the rack's structure came from a man—Number Nine—I brought home who, despite his dull, flavorless personality, had the most vibrant shade of lime I'd ever seen.

He spread across the canvas like butter.

However . . . the yellow in the handle of that vacuum cleaner could have been a shade darker to accentuate the warm undertone of the blue in the background. The rose in that cloud could have benefitted from further detailing; maybe the petals shaded in a certain way to suggest a cherub face plucked straight from the nightmare of a children's show, someone always watching. The red from Number Seven, that purple—my *god* that purple was lovely—and the orange. I can still smell her citrus perfume. The blue of the blender is only store-bought, but now I'm wondering if Number Ten's blue would have changed the entire composition of this piece. *Shit.* It's too late for that now, isn't it. *Is it?* I could find someone else with a similar blue. Not the exact same, but similar. I could sneak the color in, paintbrush hidden within my blazer pocket. Just a stroke, a single dollop. I could—

"Excuse me?"

My inner workings halt, a momentary pause in the whirlwind of my thoughts.

"Excuse me, sir?"

Is she speaking to me?

There's a light tap on my shoulder, and I shudder beneath it, dreading the voice's desires. Questions. *Questions, questions, questions.* Always dumb, silly little questions I wish I didn't have to answer.

The voice chuckles. "I know you can hear me."

Is she serious? Has the civilized concept of privacy become lost on everyone?

I turn to address the voice, the tip of my forked tongue dipped in venom, then immediately swallow my words.

She stands before me. The one from yesterday morning. The one from the alleyway and my dreams. Her color floats around her like a cloak made up of multitudes. A portal into another world. This close, that color, that divine, unprecedented color, brings tears to my eyes. I could cry. I could piss myself, lie down on this hardwood floor, and shrivel into dust.

"Did you hear me?"

"What?" I say. I plead. *What could I possibly give you?*

"Are you the artist?" she asks, pointing a noncommittal finger at my work.

My eye twitches. My palms grow clammy and my throat quivers. "Why, yes. Yes, I am." I chuckle, but it comes out insincere. Lackluster and diffident. "How did you know?"

"There's a tiny picture of you there on that plaque." I'm staring above her head. I wonder if she notices. I wonder if she notices my internals crumbling. "It's in black and white, but I can tell." I can't meet her eyes. I can't for many reasons. I simply *can't*. "I also overheard you speaking to that woman."

"Is that so?"

"Yes . . . and . . . to be honest, I caught you following me yesterday."

"What?"

Our eyes meet. I intake a sharp breath, not just from what she's said but from a further realization. Her eyes . . . they're the same color. That same deep, dark, oil-slick color.

"I said, I saw your lecture yesterday."

A false alarm. I swallow. "Is that so?"

Her eyebrow lifts and the corner of her mouth lifts with it into a crooked smile. "You're repeating yourself."

"Is that—" I bite my tongue. A shiver runs through my system. I roll my shoulders back and breathe. "My apologies. You caught me off guard."

"Famous artists aren't used to social interactions?"

I manage a fraction of a smile. I'll shift to autopilot. I'll pretend she's no one. No one important at all.

"What can I help you with?" I ask.

Her gaze moves about the room, then returns to me. "I'm new to this city."

"Welcome, then."

"I don't know much about it. Not yet, at least."

"There's much to learn and love."

"Yes, a lot to explore. But I'm scared of getting lost."

"Maps are good for that reason."

Within her dark color are pockets of duo-chromatic shift that pucker then abate like the working organs of a living animal. Browns and mulled purples. Multitudes upon polychromatic multitudes. She frowns, crosses her arms, and I've reasoned that I am a jackass.

"I get lost even with a map." She sighs and looks toward the ceiling, thinking. "I saw a theme park of sorts in the distance this morning. A Ferris wheel above the building tops. Do you know it?"

"The boardwalk," I breathe.

"What was that?"

"The boardwalk. I'd take you there. If you'd like."

Now she smiles wide and alluring. She tilts to the side and looks past me. The angle is so dismissive. I cast my eyes downward and note she is in a yellow slip the color of sunshine. It complements the undertones of her skin.

"So these are all yours?" she asks.

I turn to the collection and nod.

"You like colors."

This makes me laugh, loud and proud so that all in the gallery take fleeting peeks in our direction.

"What's so funny?"

"I'm an artist," I say. "Of course I like colors."

"That's not always true."

In a greater context, I admit, she would be right.

"I see the appliances and furnishings," she says. "Just barely. So you wanted an illusion? You wanted people to second-guess what they saw."

I scoff. "You read the plaque."

She squints to read. "That's not what the plaque says at all, is it?"

I blink and turn to read it myself. She's right again. It's about my attention to color and artistic style. My history and a list of my past exhibitions. Highlights of my most famous paintings. A note at the bottom that states I am exclusive to this gallery.

Embarrassment floods me.

She sneers. "I think you could do better."

Before I can react, the gallery owner pops her head out of her office. She approaches with her hands raised high above her head, face flushed.

"Void!" she says. "I am so sorry to keep you waiting!"

I think it's something in my facial expression that makes her stop midstride, warns her not to come any closer. She takes half a step back and smiles uncomfortably.

"A friend of yours?" she asks.

I turn to this woman whose name I don't even know, whose only quality I am truly aware of is the color of something she can't perceive. But she is unfazed. She sticks out her hand for the gallery owner to shake and when they make contact, she says:

"Zahra. Zahra Saeed. I'm Mr. Void's new friend."

"Oh," the gallery owner says, taking her hand back and

holding it to her chest. "Oh!" she says again with more enthusiasm, more recognition. "I didn't know you had such beautiful friends, Void." She turns to me as if for an explanation.

And what could I possibly tell her?

"We are going to the boardwalk today," Zahra says.

"Are you now? Well, that's wonderful! Void, you should have told me you had plans."

When I find myself unable to respond, Zahra does so for me.

"Yes, he's very busy. Not great at communicating, is he?"

At this, the gallery owner bursts into laughter. Zahra laughs along with her at the joke I am the butt of. "No, so true. Not at all." She wipes a thin tear from her eye and flicks her wrist as though to shoo us away. "Go on now, then, enjoy yourselves."

There are butterflies in my stomach whose wings are made of fiberglass. They slash at the mesentery keeping my insides in place. My heart drops with the gallery owner's wink, and then she is gone, vanishing back into her office like a lion to its den.

"Wow," Zahra says. "It's like you've never spoken to more than one person at a time."

I glare at her. I think about lashing out. I witness her color all over again and the tension in my system releases, if only by a touch.

"You talk a lot," I reply. "And like I said, you caught me off guard."

She grins as though this pleases her, this agency she has over me.

I inhale and try to reset. Try to paint on a charming smile, try to keep my cool. Inch by inch. Step by step. I can't slip up and I can't be too eager.

No color is worth the risk.

"So, the boardwalk?" I ask. "I actually know this great spot—"

She grabs my wrist. Her touch is warm and soft and pleasant in all the ways one would want. She guides me out of the gallery. I follow her without objection.

~

She has no idea where she's going. She takes me down streets and alleyways, around corners and bends, all the while chirping on about how lovely the day is. How bright and warm the sun is on her skin and how where she comes from everything is so bleak in comparison.

Her color shifts. It winks at me. Sweat stipples my skin. I'm not sure what is happening. My mind lags, as if in some parallel universe where I'd take my seat in an office chair across from the gallery owner. Where I'd discuss my art and nothing but my art. Yet here I am, wind on my face, legs pumping to keep up.

Zahra laughs at the name of a city street. She counts the pigeons on telephone lines. She comments on how the bakery nearby vents the scent of freshly baked bread and how wonderful it is for a street to smell of warmth while the sun radiates at its peak. *She* is radiant, brilliant to the point of blinding, and I know I am the only one who can see her color yet everyone we pass stops and squints at her with adoration and a dash of confusion. Like they sense she is something special. Like they know she is a once-in-a-lifetime thing. And she is, isn't she? That's why I'm here. Why I've allowed myself to be carried so far.

But so am I.

And I must remind myself, *no color is worth the risk.*

No color is worth my own downfall.

~

It is not until I rip the metaphorical reins from Zahra's eager fingers and steer us toward a cab that we arrive at the boardwalk. She spins in circles, trying to take in everything all at once, and I think about offering her the bluff's view once again, but she sees the teacup ride and squeals.

"That looks *fun!*"

I ask her if she feels the ride is entirely necessary and she snaps back at me to grow up. I can't help myself from laughing in her face.

"Grow up? *Me?* On the *teacup ride*?!"

She sticks her tongue out and I ponder how much pressure it would take to bite the muscle off. If I could use her own teeth as a paper cutter. To truly feel her tongue against mine could I swallow it whole? Would I? How would it feel to consume a piece of her?

Then I think about the teacup ride Zahra is so eager to get on. For all my time lurking on this boardwalk, I have never once ridden a ride.

I pay and we take our seats in what is essentially a faded multicolored bowl. I feel a dazzling sense of humiliation that opposes Zahra's mood. We grip the wheel between us, which I can only imagine has been touched by an unfathomable number of dirty hands. Once the ride starts, Zahra spins with all her might and I am taken by surprise, instantly struck by motion sickness. The centripetal force pulls her color inward so that it nearly touches my head, and I think I am about to weep. I try to shut my eyes, but it hurts even more not to see.

When we are off the ride, I stumble, and Zahra slings my arm across her shoulders until I find my balance.

"Okay, my choice now," I say.

I turn to the Ferris wheel, watching its rotating colors in awe, and wonder what the world below would look like at its peak.

Zahra looks on with me. Her grip on me weakens. She turns to the remaining rides—the flyer, the rollercoaster, the slingshot— and pales. Her chest inflates and her foot moves forward, but then she stops and shrinks back into herself.

"How about we play the games?" she offers.

I furrow my brow. "You don't want to ride anything anymore?"

She shakes her head, trying to mask a nervous swallow. "You're not feeling well."

I laugh with indignation. "I'm not feeling well because *you* wanted to spin the teacups back and forth."

Her eyes glass over and my smile falls. Her voice drops an octave, solemn but accepting. "Would riding it make you happy?"

I turn to the Ferris wheel, its colors brilliant yet unreachable above me. I turn to her, such a brutal thing with such a large bite. But something is off. Something she will not admit.

"No," I lie. "It wouldn't."

"I see."

She leads us through the gaming kiosks. We toss rings over rows of soda bottles, shoot basketballs into oval hoops, and throw darts at half-inflated balloons. All we manage to win is a small plush zebra the size of a fist.

Impelled by an all-consuming exuberance from staring into the pit of Zahra's color for far too long, I get down on one knee and beg for her to accept the zebra—exclaim that should she not, should she reject my gift, I would simply perish. She giggles, tells me to shut up, and takes the stuffed animal. I smile.

We share a bag of popcorn and with kernels stuck between my teeth, I wonder if her color would taste like deep-fried Oreos.

~

We walk along the edge of the boardwalk to our next game, something Zahra spotted at the entrance having to do with miniature fishing poles. A teenage girl walks toward us, her awful color of self-pity strobing through a series of similarly awful colors. She's inebriated, which is further evident by the fact that she cannot keep her body upright, stumbling this way and that.

In a fit of glee, Zahra tosses her zebra into the air. The wind carries it forward. She skips ahead to catch it in the bucket of popcorn.

And when the teenage girl smacks into Zahra, knocking her off her feet, I am already there. The zebra drops, hitting the boardwalk planks without a sound. The popcorn drops, burying the stuffed animal in buttery kernels. Zahra does not drop. Her feet spill over the boardwalk edge, threatening to dump her out onto the blazing sand four feet below, but I've caught her by the waist.

The girl stumbles, grins, laughs at what she's done. Her cackles die short when she trips over my outstretched foot. She's too drunk to stop her fall. It's like watching a lone domino topple over. When her face meets the planks, I relish in the satisfying *crunch*.

Once I'm sure Zahra is settled on her feet, I attend to the girl, who is now screaming and writhing on the boardwalk. When she turns over, I see that her nose is broken. Because of her bilious color, it is difficult to distinguish if what's oozing out from the eviscerated bridge is blood or vomit. I figure it's all the same pain. I extend a hand and offer her a wry smile.

"Are you all right, miss? You should watch where you're going."

And perhaps if you hadn't laughed, your face would still be intact.

She whimpers and reaches toward me, eyes pleading, using her other hand to cover her mangled face. The crowd watches on with looks of worry, and I wonder if the girl feels she's receiving the pity she so deserves.

Another hand, thicker and meatier, comes into view to swat

mine away. I look up and come face to face with a red-hot rage.

"You got a problem, bro?"

I shake my head and take a step back. "No, not at all. She fell."

A sunburnt boy reeking of vodka and the sour tang of energy drinks looks from me to the girl still supine on the boardwalk. He picks her up, crushing her against his chest, and approaches me with what I know is the intent to fight. But his color brightens while hers darkens with pain.

I don't even bother to curl my fingers into a fist.

The girl shrieks. It takes a moment for him to register the screams coming from within his meaty cocoon. By holding her so tightly, he's further squished her face between his muscles, her sensitive flesh pressurized beneath, shattered cartilage rubbing together with agonizing friction.

"It fucking hurts!" she cries. *"It hurts it hurts it hurts!"*

The boy panics. Her shrieks are so horrid he has no choice but to shuffle away, pink in the face, to a nearby medical tent. I watch them go, and when the crowd swallows the duo, I turn back to Zahra with a grin.

"Did you see—?"

My smug expression instantly drops. My eyes widen.

She is hunched over, facing the edge of the boardwalk, the precipice that almost took her to the sand below. Her hair dangles so that I can't see her face, but I can see the motions of her body. Her shoulders heave, and with every rise her color does not change but grows, a cloud gathering mass, a spreading shadow.

"Zahra?"

At the sound of my voice, her heaving stops. The balloon of color deflates. She bends and picks up the zebra, bits of popcorn falling from its fur.

Zahra spins around and smiles at me. Her color returns to its previous size, but it leaves behind a trace of something in her eyes. Something no longer shocked but . . . uncomfortable. A hint of distress.

"Would you like to go to the bluff now?" she asks.

I nod, and an impulse tells me to offer her my arm. She takes it and we walk. The Ferris wheel looms over us in the distance, strobing, and I wonder how Zahra would have looked at its peak.

"Would you like . . ."

She furrows her brow when I don't finish, then asks, "What?"

I shake my head and say through an awkward smile, "Would you like my number?"

Her bottom lip pouts. She turns her gaze straight ahead. "I don't have my phone on me."

"What?"

"I forgot it at home. I'm very forgetful."

"I see."

"I can give you my number."

"Okay," I say. "Later."

She nods.

We reach the bluff and I'm dizzy. I think this was building up. A motion sickness not just from the ride, but from the day. I feel outside my own body. A strange whiplash, like the world is, without warning, moving pieces that best fit around me. I am not a superstitious person. I believe in free will. I believe life is a series of unexplainable, unrelated events that I am meant to navigate with divine precision, but suddenly it feels the opposite. It feels like something is working me down the universe's easiest maze, and I'm excited for the end because the outcome seems worth the manipulation.

Zahra looks out and squeals her excited squeal.

"It's beautiful!" she exclaims.

And I watch her and I try not to drop right then and there as my nervous system sways with the waves that breach the bluff.

She turns to me, her eyes that color no one else could possibly see—not the way *I* see—and I wonder . . . if not like this, then how does the world perceive her? What do they see without the ability to see all of her? Whatever it is, it is a loss. It is a true loss not to know her as I do.

"Are you happy?" she asks.

I scoff and say, "How could I not be?"

She shrugs and says nothing more and we both turn to face the bluff, our forearms resting along the cold metal rail.

As the waves crash, I wonder if, unbeknownst to me, she can see me too.

~

We are in my studio.

We are in my studio, and she does not have a phone.

We are in my studio, and she walks barefoot across the vinyl tarp, her soles traversing these floors like she was destined to take these steps. Her color paints the empty canvases of my mind and I imagine all that I could accomplish. All the ways I could make use of her. She's eyeing the pieces I have righted, rehung, and touched up.

"Here's where the—how did you put it?—*spectral magic* happens," I say with a smirk. "I hope it's as impressive as you imagined."

"Phoenixes?" she asks.

I nod. "I'm considering them as the subject for my next installment. Although at this rate it looks like I'll have no other choice."

She steps around an easel, heel to toe, head swaying like she's floating in water. "Why is that?"

I shrug. "They're all I care to paint as of late. Phoenixes in unexpected places, anywhere other than rising from the ashes. I can't get the image out of my head . . ."

She hums, lips pursed, blinking slowly as she continues weaving her way through my studio. "What do you think about zebras?" she asks, tossing the stuffed animal from the boardwalk in my direction.

I fumble to catch it and laugh, rolling it between my hands, peering into its beady little plastic eyes. "I think they're fine."

"Would you ever paint them?"

"Probably not, no."

"Why not?"

I glance at her, then turn back to the zebra. I press my thumbs into its soft belly. "They're bland."

"How are they *bland*?"

I shake my head, run my tongue over my teeth. What would she know?

"They're bland because they're only ever black and white and they eat grass."

"You painted normal household items in eccentric colors. Why not zebras?"

I scoff, then gape at her, wide-eyed, annoyed at how she could so unabashedly fail to understand. *Eccentric colors?!* Those colors are a glance into my world. An assault of pigmentation so visceral some need to step away. And still, there is so much more to it than that.

"*That* was a play on the mundane," I tell her, "on what we see every day. How the shapes can remain the same, but we're caught off guard when the vibrancy shifts in a different direction or the palette changes hue. It symbolizes our helplessness to color as a heuristic, color as a means to navigate quickly through day-to-day life. Zebras are neither mundane nor interesting enough to show to an audience." I lightly backhand the zebra's snout as if that further proves my point. "Besides, I think the kitschy neon color scheme—sorry, *eccentric colors*—on zoo animals has been done one too many times before."

Zahra stands before me. Her expression offers me nothing. My heart has accelerated, and I struggle to understand how I've become so irate.

"Hmm," she says.

I think about running my fingertips over her collarbones, dipping my knuckles beneath her color, curling my hands around her neck. That calms me down, but not enough.

"What?" I ask.

Her eyes roll in her skull, gazing once again at all my work. Now she smiles, but it's cloying.

"What?" I take a step forward.

She looks back at me and shrugs. "You're not one to take on a challenge."

"Not one to . . . ?"

I drop the zebra. It bounces pathetically against the tarp before lying inert, dead. Not one to take on a challenge? *Me?* My entire life has been a challenge. But I don't tell her that as she observes me with a smirk, knowing she's made an exhibition of pushing the buttons that so easily access my rage. Her color sways and undulates and winks at me, and I realize I am slightly hunched over as if readying to lunge, and that wouldn't be wise in this situation. Not wise at all.

I need to think.

She has no phone, but people saw us together. The *gallery owner* saw us together. Typically, that would be a huge no-no for me, but risk be damned. The universe so kindly returned this color to my possession, I cannot possibly let it get away again. It would drive me off the edge. I could stretch this out for a while longer. I could date her in the shadows, try not to be seen together. Hope that people will forget her face in connection with mine.

I close my eyes and breathe, turn my grimace into charm. When I look at her again, I do it with warmth, with affectionate understanding.

"Fair enough," I say. "Maybe there is something to this whole zebra thing."

Her color glistens as she steps toward me, her movement fluid. There is something uniquely ethereal to her presence beyond just her color. Something torturously holy. My lips part and I find myself leaning back. She wraps her arms around my neck, presses her face into my chest, breathes me in. I hesitate, arms open, questioning my next move, before I give in. I hug her and I am lost in her color. In the shroud of oil-slick shimmer surrounding me.

I tear up.

No color is worth the risk, but losing her would mean devastation.

She pulls away and upon noticing my tears kisses my eyes, licks the salt from my skin.

"Why are you crying?" she asks.

"I'm not."

The lie is blatant, but she smiles anyway. She leads me to the center of my studio, where she places her hand on my chest. Her pressure guides me down, down, down, until I am sitting, until I am lying on my back. I watch her stand above me, staring at me, and I feel I am in a strange place. A place I've never been before. I wonder about this place. I wonder if I like it here. She is taking off her dress, sliding the baked-sand-and-sea-salt-scented fabric over her honeyed ribs, her chest, her hair, and as it comes off, she hits the corner of my central easel. The painting clatters; the phoenix trembles in its frame.

The palette knife falls not too far from me. Within arm's reach.

"Would you paint me?" she asks.

Naked, she lowers herself onto my lap, straddles my waist. Her inner thighs are warm as she pushes against me.

"Yes," I say. "Of course I would." *If only you knew.*

She untucks me from my pants, shoves her underwear to the side.

"I'm not too *bland* for you?"

"No."

It dawns on me then that I am beneath her. Not on top. Not holding her down so I can keep her in place while I watch her flare up. Yet I am not panicking. I am calm. Somehow I am certain the view will be all the more heavenly from below.

"How can you know?" she asks.

"I just know."

She leans down and I am blinded, her neck covering my face. But I can feel. I can feel myself slip inside her. She feels slick and tender, like a warm wave rushing to meet me over and over again. A blanket just out of the dryer. Her breath hits my skin in rhythm with her rise and fall, her moans soft and sweet. When she lifts herself, continuing this motion from a different angle, I am not surprised that her color remains the same. That it does not strobe. I'm actually happy. Thankful, even. Thankful I get to witness it from this position, my spine against the very tarps I have used to swaddle so many dead bodies. Her movement accelerates, plunging faster, and I clench against the fluttering in my head. I place my hands around her thighs, moving with her. Her color ascends and descends until it is all around her, all around me, a globe of our own making.

No color is worth the risk. But she is here, and we are in this secluded corner of the universe, discovering new terrain and sights never before seen.

No one would know.

No one would ever see us.

"The entire world deserves to see you," I declare aloud.

Her pressure builds and suddenly I can't take it. It feels like a trap, like an iron maiden made of painfully dull spikes. It feels as though stars live here, kissing my skin with sweet fire, and if I don't get out soon I might suffocate.

But I must stay.

I must stay for her.

She rolls her shoulders back, arches her spine, raises her chin to the ceiling. Her breasts are puckered with glistening sweat as they jounce up and down, nipples carving lines into the unsuspecting air. My hands find her hips, her waist, the ridges of her ribs, then fall back. My knuckles hit the tarp above my head. Something clatters.

The palette knife.

I reach for it, tiptoe my fingers around the handle, caress the temptation.

She's moaning, running her hands through her hair. She is

here but also not here, not watching me, completely unaware. Her color flutters. It winks at me, waiting, anticipating; it grows richer, hotter, denser, wet and heavy. I'm sweating, I'm drowning. My chest, filled with fiberglass butterflies, hyperventilates from the pleasure and the immense agony. Supernovas form beneath my skin in the places she leaves her touch.

I grab the palette knife.

Her color beckons me. The blade is in her chest before I can even process that I have moved. My fingers are curled around the handle, and she has come to a rest. The earth has stopped turning. The oceans have found an eldritch stillness. I am horrified. I am elated. Reflexively, I drag the blade down—down, down, down, down into the depths of something unknown . . .

I am surprised she does not scream. She only sits, her neck contorted as she stares long and hard at the ceiling.

The slice furls open like a set of curtains. It weeps. My eyes glisten as liquid knowledge the color of wicked obscurity rushes forth. She spills out onto my thighs, pools beneath my belly, gets caught in the currents of my muscles. Her color drips between our legs and coats us in a heated film. Those butterflies with their deadly wings fill my heart, my throat, and tear at my insides with sadistic hedonism. I could swallow her whole. I could drink her, fill my very veins with her.

She shudders, and my eyes shoot up from the center of her split chest to the underside of her chin. Something leaks down either side of her face, and I register them as tears made from the same color as within. They trail down her neck, down her shoulders and arms, flickering like galaxies.

She tilts her head toward me, her eyes now strobing through every color of this earth, its heavens and hells, and it's like standing before oncoming headlights. She smiles wide, purloins control of the blade, and slips it out.

Something is happening.

Something is happening to her.

There's a high-pitched whine, and it takes a moment to realize *I* am the one whimpering, as the damage I've done stitches itself back up, inch by inch, her flesh joining together, threads of skin fusing back into one, sealing her shut.

She drops the palette knife. She moves once again, undeterred—up and down, up and down—her blood reaching into places it was previously blocked from. I grab at her stomach, pressing that color into our skin, finger-painting a living canvas, and she grabs at the backs of my hands. She guides my touch to her face, wipes away those galaxies of tears with the heel of my palm, and I think about her bones. If they're made up of dying stars. If they're made from the same stuff that keeps space suspended.

And the thought passes me so sweetly amidst this world-shattering violence:

If I am a void, then she is utter totality.

~

I wake in the dark, Zahra's arm draped across my chest. We are still on the vinyl tarps, naked and blood-soaked.

My eyes are on fire.

I lurch up from the floor, tempted to press the palms of my hands into my eye sockets. Tempted to snuff out that stinging pain with some pressure. But it won't do any good.

This is what I get for sleeping with my contacts in.

I have probably woken up Zahra by now, although I am unsure. It is dark, and from what I can see through my veneer of pain, she lies still amongst the shadows.

With a grunt, I jump to my feet and rush naked to the bathroom. My reflection shows me that I am stained with color, a white dove caught in an oil spill. My eyes are utterly bloodshot, the contacts slipping from my corneas like ice cream from a cone. I rinse my hands with warm water and soap, then pull the contacts out with trembling fingers—careful not to rush—and drop them into their lens case. The pain subsides. My eyes are clear, black dots against an expansive white background. I lower my head, happy with the comfort.

"Void?"

My heart stops. My eyes widen, my pupils dilate, muscles tense.

"Void, is everything okay?"

My hands grip the porcelain lip of the basin, willing it to crack. Willing for a distraction. Zahra is behind me, in the doorway of the bathroom. If I look up, she'll see. If I turn around, she'll see. If I try to leave the room with my eyes closed, she'll stop me.

A touch against my back, caring and light.

"Void, what's wrong?"

~

My eyes were first seen by someone four years ago. I was visiting a small town in Vermont for a mixture of pleasure and business. I'd been in a rut creation-wise and needed a break from the city. From the gallery owner's demands and general ruckus. I packed myself into an Airbnb, laid out several different sketch pads, and externalized my stream of consciousness onto their pages, switching pads every ten minutes to keep the creative flow going. This is my process, much like how writers will freewrite to overcome writer's block.

It was a particularly sunny day—I remember the rays against the light wood floorboards were blinding, but I kept the curtains drawn so the home's glass mobiles cast rainbows across my arms and sketchpads. It was beautiful even if it hurt.

I was in the middle of adding structure to sketchpad number three when I heard a woman's laugh, loud and hysterical. I glanced up and saw from the living room windows the woman in question, phone pressed against her ear, leash wrapped around her free hand. At the end of the leash was a small dog, some corgi mix glowing with the most interesting shade of yellow I'd ever seen. Something like aureolin mixed with curiosity and adventure.

Entranced, I stood from my sketchpads, intrigue grabbing ahold of me.

The dog was worming its way out of its collar while its owner stared into the sky, still laughing, unaware of the escape artist. She had some pale shade of pink mixed with a color like envy but seeded deeper. I didn't particularly care for it; it was an ugly color.

But that corgi's yellow . . .

By the time I was out the door, the dog had managed to squirm out of its collar and was trotting down the street. At the end of that street was an on-ramp to a highway I'd heard many a car zip through over those past few days. And the thought of that tart yellow splattered uselessly across the asphalt brought me absolutely no pleasure.

Still, the dog trotted on, too brave or too stupid to notice.

I hurried my step. The woman behind caught on, and with high-pitched panic shouted, "No! *Russell, no!*"

But she was too far away, and I was running now because the dog, in a zing of playfulness, was ecstatic at the prospect of being chased. Its stubby legs neared the on-ramp and I thought of all I could paint with that color.

The sun, a field of corn or wheat, strawberry-blond hair.

The owner was wailing now.

A star, a smattering of honey, a slice of cheese.

Cars zoomed by at sixty miles per hour, unaware of the one-foot-tall animal nearing their tires.

A lemon tree.

Before the dog could jump down the curb, I scooped it up into my arms. It yelped in surprise as I tugged it away from those skid marks, into the air. I held it by the armpits, staring into its clueless eyes, pink tongue lolling from the side of its mouth.

"Oh, thank you! Thank you so much!"

Hands reached out from behind me to grab the dog. I held on for a moment, squeezing the thing like its color might ooze between my fingers and I could safely transport a piece of it home with me. It yelped again, this time from pain.

"What are you doing?" the corgi's owner asked. "Hey, give him back, all right?"

Remembering myself, I released. The dog was taken from my grip and the owner cooed in relief.

"Seriously, thank you so much. Stupid dog. He would've just run right into traffic."

I turned to her. Her face was pressed against the top of her dog's head, breathing in its fur. Only now did I realize how young she was, no older than nineteen, and the envy had left her color, revealing a pure rose pink. I'd never been one to note color combinations when I'm not the one putting them to canvas, but the two of them together, curled in loving embrace, slobbering kisses and all, was beautiful.

She turned to me, eyes glossy, ready to be enamored with her rescuer. But when she saw me, she stopped. Her expression froze. Her color darkened. She seemed to go limp and had to regrip her dog to keep from dropping it.

It dawned on me then with terrible dread what I had done.

I'd spent the entirety of this trip in solitude, my typical morning routine abandoned. And this girl was staring at my horrible eyes in broad daylight. No contacts, only pinpricks of dilating abyss.

She ran away from me screaming, dog yipping like a rabid hound in her arms.

Immediately, I packed my things and left, swearing I'd never come back to Vermont on the off chance I'd run into that girl again and have to face her expression of absolute disgust.

I felt like a nightmare. A monster.

~

Now I've brought that dread home with me. It's coming—all I have to do is turn around and face Zahra. And when she sees me, she will no longer see a beautiful painter but a monster, and she too will run away, her color forever lost.

I'm searching for a way out. A way to avoid this. Gears grind in my mind. Zahra. Here, behind me. After . . .

Wait.

Could it be? Was it a dream? Had I not driven my blade into her? Had she not split open with a smile and climaxed against her own blood? Is she even truly behind me right now? Or is this voice a part of some waking dream, her lifeless body on the floor of my studio, rotting away?

I spin around. Zahra retracts her hand like my motion might rip it clean off. She takes a step back, staring at me, wide-eyed, one hand behind the doorframe, and I think: This is the moment. This is the moment she takes off screaming. I'll have to chase after her. I'll have to hold her down and knock her out, start all over again.

Instead, her eyes soften.

Instead she asks, "Is everything all right in here?"

She looks about the bathroom as if searching for an answer to my being in this place without her. I regrip the sink behind me like it's a life raft. Like letting go would lead to my immediate drowning.

"Yes," I respond. "Everything's fine."

"Are you sure?"

I smile tightly. "I'm sure. My eyes were just a little irritated, so I came in here to wash them out."

Perhaps she hadn't seen. She just woke up; her sight needs to adjust, and there are shadows in this room. I open my eyes wider, just slightly, willing her to notice.

She scrunches her face, her stare roaming from one eye to the next. Back and forth, seeing nothing out of the usual. Satisfied, she shrugs and pouts her lips.

"Want to come back to bed?"

"Bed?" I scoff, biting back a laugh. She looks hurt, and a pang hits deep where I find regret. "You know, I do have an *actual* bed. Not just a floor piled with tarps."

Once again, Zahra shrugs. "Bed is wherever I find rest."

She smiles, but there's a hint of something dark there. Her hand moves out of frame, grazing the wall outside of my bathroom with what I assume, by the sound, are her nails.

I watch her a moment, feeling the tables have turned on me, wondering when this happened. Her eyes shimmer with that oil-slick color that nearly blends into the darkness behind her. I taste the insides of my cheeks.

"I like your eyes," I say.

Her eyebrows knit together. She steps forward into the bathroom, hand swooping from behind the doorframe to a concealed place against her spine.

"Really?" she says in surprise, the color of her irises spiraling around and around. My head grows light. "No one's ever told me that before. They're just brown."

I could break the sink right now I'm gripping it so hard.

I swallow. "Brown can be a very beautiful color in its own right."

"A famous painter should know," she says with a giggle. "Now, come back to bed."

She moves her hand from her back and presses it against my chest. Something long and hard digs into my sternum, and I realize it wasn't her nails. She was holding something this entire time.

My palette knife.

"I'm hungry for another round," she says.

I look from the bloodstained knife back to her and I believe her. I truly believe she is hungry, something dreadful deep down inside of her starved for far too long.

"What are you?" I ask, unaware the question ever formed in my thoughts.

She bites her bottom lip, eyes large and hypnotizing.

"I'm yours."

~

We are back on the tarps, and this time I am on top, plunged into her, both my cock and my palette knife, shredding her apart, watching her skin come undone, her color spilling out across our bodies with such newfound vivacity. For every slash I exact, there is a moan and a protest of healing. I could spend an eternity ruining something that is infinitely regenerative. Invincible. All mine.

And all I can think about are her words and her blood and that dog that would have run into traffic with a smile had I let it.

~

I wake up in a puddle of sunlight and color. I thought it would be warm, but it is not; her color is room temperature. Parts of it have coagulated, forming lumps, and there is a film around my skin like fat from old meat. Despite its texture it is still beautiful, although probably not proper to harvest for art.

Fresh is always better.

I flex my muscles, stretch my spine, and turn over. Zahra rests beside me, eyes closed, a slight smile on her lips. For a moment I think she is dead, but that thought is immediately squashed when I see the rise and fall of her ribcage. She is as naked as I am, coated in the same way by her color, her skin smooth and without blemish.

Without scars.

All that color surrounds her unconscious body. She is an anomaly. An art piece. Like something I might capture, immortalize in clay and paint, and savor all to myself.

I grow hard. The space behind my molars fills with tangy-sweet drool. As if sensing my arousal, Zahra's eyes slowly blink open. When she sees me, her smile stretches. Fiberglass wings cut at my insides, filling me with warmth.

"Hello," she whispers.

"Good morning," I say, and brace for her reaction to all that is around us. Surely she sees blood where I see her color. But she is unbothered, calm, relaxed—happy, even.

She is dead. Her movements are a figment of my imagination. She cannot be real. It is not possible. *She* is not possible.

I lean in to kiss her forehead, press my lips hard against her skin. It is warm.

No, she is not dead. She is very much alive.

She groans, stretches, and props herself up onto her elbows. "We've made quite a mess, haven't we?"

I stare silently, and when I do not respond, she turns to me with a hungry grin.

"Shall we have at it again?"

It's not a question; it's a premonition. She is already on top of me, grinding her hips into mine. I place my hands on her waist and shudder as she slides me inside. This time I do not grab for the palette knife. This time I enjoy her as she is, whole, not split open and bleeding out onto my floor. A kind of organic interaction I have never once before enjoyed. And I do find it wonderful how I enjoy it. How the weight of her intimacy does not hurt.

She continues her grinding motion, but I notice it is less passionate, less excited. Her face dims as time passes and she realizes I am making no move for the palette knife.

But I am too tired, and the sheer volume of this color will overwhelm me, make me nauseous from the serotonin high. From how deep the vast unknown is between us, an abyss I am too fatigued to peer into right now. I can only take so much.

She, on the other hand, seems to desire so much more.

~

When we are both done and sated—although *sated* seems like a distant concept for Zahra—we gather ourselves to wash all manner of fluids from our bodies. I offer her the shower alone, but she pulls me in with her, and I'm glad she does. Seeing her color through water droplets is like watching a kaleidoscope consume prisms. When we exit the shower, she towel-dries her hair with a yawn, and I notice her color seems to weaken into a muted glow. I have the extra steps of putting on my brown contacts and rubbing rouge onto my cheeks, all the while self-conscious of her stare. She doesn't seem to question nor mind; I, however, mind how little this disturbs her.

Her dress was ruined by color, although I'd argue the opposite. I lend her a pair of jeans and a T-shirt, all black, while we run her clothes through the wash. I had my theories, and I was right—her color looks more vibrant against the dark clothing, and seeing her small frame carry the same fabric that is too tight on me is appealing.

Her stomach grumbles. I lift an eyebrow in response.

"Hungry?" I ask.

She nods. "Ravenous."

There is a diner not too far away from my building. I ponder the risk of being seen there together, but she has weaseled her way out of death twice now and I have the suspicion this pattern will continue. Hiding our relationship seems no longer necessary.

Plus, I'd just love to watch that color eat.

When we arrive, I order us coffee while we peruse our menus. I hold my menu just below eye level so I can watch her over the laminated food options I do not need to read. Her face is scrunched in concentration, lips moving around dish names and ingredients, her color growing with each sip of coffee. She places the mug down, taps the porcelain once, twice, then lifts it for another sip.

The waiter approaches and asks what he can get for us.

Zahra smiles large and wide as if to show off the teeth she can easily consume this meal with. "I'll have steak and eggs, please. Steak, medium rare, eggs, sunny side up."

"And for you, sir?" the waiter asks.

"Greek yogurt," I tell him. "The fruit bowl, a side of hash browns, and a glass of orange juice, please."

The waiter nods. His eyes linger on me like maybe he recognizes me, and only now do I notice the purple color he's been carrying around as though I'd been blinded to it by something stronger. Purple . . . and such a rare hue. Like crushed murex shells.

When he leaves, Zahra grunts in disapproval. I return my attention to her color, where it belongs.

"Seems like a light breakfast for a muscular guy like you," she says.

I shrug. "It's enough."

"Not much protein. You're not a big meat eater?"

"I'm a vegetarian," I say, thumbing the handle of the coffee mug.

"Ah," Zahra remarks.

There's a moment of silence that says neither of us cares much for small talk. *How are you liking this weather? What have you been up to? What's new?* It's not small talk I want. I want to ask her questions, so many questions. The first being, Why are you not dead?

Instead I ask, "So, why did you move here?"

Zahra looks at me like it's the first time. Then says, "I'm running away."

"From what?"

"Hmm, how do you put it?" She rolls her eyes, lifts her shoulders, then drops them with a smirk. "The mundane."

"The mundane?"

A hum of affirmation. "I used to work in sales." She rests her cheek on her hand and stares into her coffee. "At this little boutique store on Main Street. It wasn't much, but it was enough. Every day I'd wake up at six a.m., get ready, be at the store by seven-thirty, and open an hour later. Then at closing, I'd pack up, say goodbye to the store owner, and head home—I lived in a little apartment not too far away. But that was it. Every day for quite a few years."

"Huh." I grit my teeth.

"Yeah. We had some pretty good customers, loyal and kind, but then we had the ones I call *lost souls*. The ones who remind you the world isn't entirely rational. Once, a lady walked in with a takeout bag, something from some Italian restaurant I could smell the moment she entered. She wanted to try on some clothes, so I set up the fitting room for her. She goes in with this takeout bag, and I *see* her go in with it. She *saw* me see her go in with it. She's in there for twenty minutes, which is an absurdly long time to try on a couple shirts, and when she comes out, she shows me that all the clothing she brought in got stained with spaghetti sauce."

I must be making a face because Zahra giggles, but whatever exaggerated disbelief I express is not from her story. It's from the reality of sitting across from a girl who defines her life as mundane despite apparently being unable to die.

"Yup!" She continues, "And in this thin film of human civility we have all socially constructed, you'd think her next reaction would be to apologize and offer to pay for the damaged goods."

"I'd think so."

"No." Zahra shakes her head. "She demanded I give them to her at a discount because the clothes were clearly *damaged*."

"You're kidding."

"I'm not! She made a scene, and it was so late in the evening, I was the only one on shift at the time."

"What did you do?"

"I told her to leave the store. She could leave the clothes and not pay a dime, but I needed her to leave. She was giving me a headache."

"And what did *she* do?"

"She just kinda . . . seized up. Her face got really red and she started going off about how I didn't know how to run a business. How I was ridiculous for taking back damaged goods without receiving a dime rather than giving them to her at a discount. And then she ended it all by saying, 'Why are you like this?' " Zahra releases her coffee mug and clasps her hands together. "What a strange thing to say to someone, don't you think? 'Why are you like this?' Like she *knew* me."

Her eyes grow distant; her color pulses. I remain quiet, watching the aura steady around her. The aura that bleeds from her like a crown of imploding stars.

"I left after that," she says. "I just packed up my things, gave myself a couple days to pick a new place, a new plan, and I left."

"Just like that?"

"I couldn't take it anymore, you know? The routine, the same rotation over and over again, like the store was a revolving door for lost souls and I was a magnet." She takes another sip from her mug. "It was boring, unexciting . . . It just got old."

I nod, my thoughts processing. "And, could you remind me, what town was this in again?"

Her expression distorts, cringes, morphs into a grimace like I've somehow wounded her. And for once, I find that reaction more curious than any possible color change.

The waiter interrupts with our food, two arms and two plates descending upon our table, hiding Zahra's face.

"Here you both go!"

When the waiter removes himself from my view, Zahra's expression is no longer one of horror. She has returned to that joyous, wide-eyed image of a girl who thinks she is completely untouched by any darkness within or around her. She is staring at her plate, at the slab of meat and eggs soaked in the unappetizing color of survival so common to all meat products, as though she is ready to shove it all down her throat without a single chew. As though she would inhale it whole if she were alone.

"Is there anything else I can get for you?" the waiter asks.

I feel a touch on my shoulder. I look up and see him staring at me, a demure smile spread across his lips. I smile back flirtatiously, for I admire the color purple—such a royal shade—and it's an opportunity to look away from the bilious color on Zahra's plate.

"No," I say, "that will be all, thank you."

The waiter leaves, and Zahra has already severed a piece of steak and skewered it through her fork. She shoves it into her eggs, popping the embryos of each and lathering the flesh in fat. She shoves the bite into her mouth and I'm glad to see an ounce of that color swallowed, gone.

"Where were we again?" she says, taking another bite, and I can see the ugly color on her tongue between chews. My blood boils. Is she doing this on purpose? "Oh, yes! Silly people asking silly questions." She carves out a third slice with the steak knife, gives it a dip, and adds to the vile mastication party between her teeth. "It was just so absurd, you know? Such a weird question to ask someone. *Why* are you like this? Hmm?" She swallows, takes another bite, chews. "I have so many stories. Most of them customer-service nightmares. Things that make you really hate people."

I feel lightheaded, like my brain might ooze out of my ears. I'll fall face-first into my fruit bowl, the flesh of those colorless fruits cold against my heated skin, if I don't maintain some semblance of control.

"Like," Zahra continues, "once—"

A train must be passing, but that can't be, because the trains here are all underground. Still, I hear the whistling. It kills the sound from my senses.

She sets the steak knife down so the pointed end of it grazes my fingertip.

How can she be talking like this? So casually, like we are two normal people having a normal conversation over a normal breakfast. As though she is something so basic, something so common in life, when that color surrounds her. When she *bleeds* that color over and over again and does not die.

My fingers, trembling, slide atop the steak knife's blade.

"Can you believe that? It's incredible what people think they can—"

Her voice fades in and out, but the blade feels cool. She hasn't reached for it again, instead using the edge of her fork to cut into the soft eggs.

"—who cares in the end? Mind you—"

I drag the blade toward me without thinking, something inside driving my body's movements. Zahra doesn't notice, too busy speaking between chews to realize my eyes are vacant. She sets her hand on the table palm down, rubbing the edge of her plate with her thumbnail.

"—and really, in the grand scheme of things, we're all meaningless."

I pick up the knife and drive it into her hand, right between the metacarpal bones of her middle and ring finger. The blade pierces through, pinning her palm to the table, burying itself into the plastic and wood beneath. Zahra's only reaction is a quiet moan, like a surprised *oomph* as she stares at me in a different light. Something surprised, then dark, then—

Hungry.

Color squeezes up and out from between the blade and her skin. It flows down her hand in ribbons. The galaxies that compose her palette shine beautifully against her in this dingy diner's lighting.

"Finally . . ."

She whispers this under her breath, just soft enough that the comment might escape me. My brow creases like a confused little boy, and then I am enraged by this fact. By my apparent stupefaction.

I pull the blade out quickly before anyone can notice, already knowing there are no security cameras in this diner—I've checked—but still, this was risky. So damn risky. I set the knife atop her plate. The steel drips and colors intermix into a vicious hue, her ethereal shade with that awful pigment of an animal's failed survival.

"We are addressing this," I say.

The wound in her hand heals, stitching itself perfectly as though with a microscopic, invisible thread. She picks up a napkin and wipes off the color, allowing for the excess to drip back onto her plate of soggy eggs and partially digested meat.

"All right," she says.

The waiter returns to ask if we need a refill on drinks. When he sees the mess of blood across the tabletop—the streaks I see as galaxies and he surely sees as swaths of brown and pink and too much red—he yelps.

Zahra assures him everything's okay. "The steak came out bloody, hon." She reaches over and places a hand on his arm, wiping herself down with the other hand as if to show there's nothing to be afraid of. No tricks up her sleeves. "I carelessly tipped the plate over. It spilled everywhere. Really, I'm fine."

He looks to the plate, the crime scene of bloodstain patterns, then to Zahra and her perfectly intact skin, and finally to me.

I wink and give him a nudge. "Everything's all right," I say, despite the monster brewing inside of me, greedy for answers. "Could we get the check, please?"

The waiter blushes, wipes his hands down his uniform, and nods. "Right. Of course."

He brings us the check. I pay, leaving behind a hefty tip and my plate of untouched melons, hashbrowns, and yogurt.

On our way back to my studio, I think about what would happen if I grabbed Zahra by the shoulders and pushed her in front of an oncoming car.

~

When I open the door to my studio, greeted by my central work in progress, that phoenix climbing out of its perpetual hole, I feel my entire lower intestinal tract drop inches into my pelvis. This is what onset inspiration feels like: a combination of euphoria and reality-shattering dread.

Zahra closes the door behind us. I store the work in progress on a shelf nearby and replace it with a blank canvas. As I gather tubes of paint, Zahra speaks.

"The truth is I have no idea why I'm like this. Why I can be cut and bled but never die. It feels good. It's the only time anything ever feels good."

I grab reds and oranges, blues and yellows, whites and beiges, smear them across my palette and mix portions together with my knife.

"I kind of knew when I was in elementary school," she continues. "All the other kids had cuts and bruises, a new one every day, every hour. Kids are glass like that, they break easily."

I outline the foundation, the system, ideas exploding in my head. I can see it already on the blank expanse, the creation to come.

"The first time I got experimental with it was in high school. I asked a boy I was dating to hit me while he fucked me. I asked him to do it harder when he gave me nothing but a weak slap, and I prodded him until I called his dick small and he broke my nose. I came immediately. He never spoke to me again."

I think about that implosion of color bursting forth from the most fragile place on the human body. Then I think about it in reverse, a vacuum returning bits of skin and bone to their place like a jigsaw puzzle, blood funneling back into healing capillaries.

"My parents never noticed—I guess they just thought I was an extremely healthy child—and I went to college without incident. That's when the binge drinking started. It was glorious. I'd go to frat parties by myself, drunk enough to behave incoherently but not drunk enough to forget. Never drunk enough to feel nothing. College parties are like vats of snakes—you just have to know which snake to take home with you."

I'm running the brush up and down the canvas now, slashing into it with zero hesitation and every ounce of bravery. I imagine the rage, the pain, the undeniable pleasure. I feel it all myself, that delicious horror.

"I'd scare them," she tells me. "Oh, *god*, would I scare them. Not because I was carrying out some perverse justice, but because I couldn't help it. It's what made my life worth living. When it was all over, they'd grow sick from it. I think parts of them died inside from seeing me like that. From seeing what they'd done to me and how I just laughed at them. How I'd smile and wave when we saw each other on campus the next day, like nothing ever happened."

The blend is magnificent, the palette of color itself a true work of art. Rainbows in reverse, arced in a field of negative afterimaging. High exposure, vibrancy—enough visual abuse to make one's eyes bleed.

"When I graduated, I had to move away. Far, far away. I'd thought about changing my name but decided it wasn't necessary. No one would hunt me down. They all wanted to forget. I carried on the same pattern in my new town, cycling through people until there were none left who would touch me."

It's starting to materialize, birth itself on this canvas. I am the divine, the guiding hand. The image has always been there, just waiting in oblivion to one day be created by me.

"I didn't leave because of those customers. I left because everyone was starting to catch on."

I see its eyes, its beak, the way it strains to overpower you.

"I'm glad I came here," Zahra tells me. "I'm glad I found you. I could sense it in you, you know? That violence. I could tell you were different."

It's a revelation. A glimpse into another dimension of the beyond.

"I could tell we were made for each other."

I don't know for how long I stand there, staring at this canvas. The pressure drops and there's a *whomp*ing in my ears—a signifier that my heart is still beating. There's a quiet *click* like the front door shutting, or maybe it's something within me locking into place. Something that derives such hedonistic delight from what I've done.

And wouldn't the addition of Zahra's color make this the quintessential masterpiece?

I turn to face her, paintbrush extended, but find she is not there.

~

It is said that Jackson Pollock's wife was a huge inspiration for his work. Lee Krasner, the renowned abstract expressionist. Her style was revolutionary. She laid canvas on the ground to paint like a true conqueror and did not shy away from raw, evocative experimentation. Her methods infected Pollock's whether he was conscious of it or not, but he only ever skyrocketed while she remained in his shadow.

It was 1956 when Pollock drove his Oldsmobile convertible at eighty miles per hour into a tree, decapitating himself. There were other casualties, but I find his manner of death to be the most memorable. Poetic, even. After the incident, Krasner fell into a deep depression.

She would not get her due recognition for her life's work, her pain and suffering, until she was seventy-five years of age.

I think about him, and I think about her, and I think about Zahra as the gallery owner's red lips move around pointless words. She has me holed up in her office, where she's trying to convince me to do more lectures, to push forward the date of the next exhibition opening. She wants me to perform an array of stunts—a photoshoot for the website, handouts, business cards, postcards of my art which patrons can purchase from a newly idealized gift shop.

Who the fuck sends postcards anymore?

Interviews, podcasts, meet and greets, tours.

"Tours?" I repeat with disdain. "Where, pray tell? You own me."

She licks the corner of her lip, thinking, then relents. "Perhaps not *tours* exactly, but you understand the point. We need more interaction between you and the world out *there*. More of your face so the viewership grows."

"The viewership *has* grown."

"Not enough."

I press my lips together, my ears catching on to a previous slip. "Who is *we*?"

The gallery owner taps her French manicured nails along her desk. Funny—just a couple days ago they were freshly lacquered with navy blue, a color nearly matching her own, and I'd wondered if she could sense it; if she is somehow self-aware.

"The shareholders," she says. "They're peeking their heads into my doors like hungry birds, and they're not happy with the grub. They think you've lost touch."

I narrow my eyes. "Lost touch?"

"They think this new collection is nothing but a weak attempt at what's been done before. I mean, 'reimagining the mundane'? I know your expertise lies in chromatics, but people . . . people want *arousal*. They want something that will push boundaries, a fearless feat. They want transcendence intermingled with a corruption that will leave them impossibly ill. Psychological violation. Awe-devouring humility. Martyrdom! Cataclysms that shake the very ground they stand on. They want to be offended. Do you understand me?"

My mouth trembles around a thousand curses, heat rising. If only my skin could blush to show it. She's spitting out buzzwords from a collection of new-age catalogs she's perused. Empty words bouncing inside of an empty skull I could crack open to collect what's not worthy of the beauty of a blank canvas.

I bite my tongue. I relax in my seat, inhale, exhale, and say, "I absolutely understand. I can assure you I have something ... *cataclysmic* ... arriving for the next installation. It will be like nothing you've ever seen."

The gallery owner seems relieved by this, like a weight has been lifted off her shoulders and she is physically lighter. Her posture lengthens; her wrinkles relax.

"I'm glad we had this talk, Void," she says with a smile. "I'm only worried for your future."

I smile back at her and wonder how difficult it would be to tear the skin from her body and reupholster it onto a frame. I imagine it would not be difficult at all.

When I leave her office, I am not surprised to see Zahra waiting for me in the gallery. She doesn't bother pretending to be interested in the art. Instead, she stands unflinchingly in the center of the room, facing the gallery owner's office, staring, waiting.

And it makes sense. In that green dress she wears, *she* is the art piece.

When she sees me, she smiles. I smile back, although the gallery owner's words are still in my ears and every muscle in my body screams at me to storm out the building. Start a tantrum, cause a scene. Instead, I join her.

We grab food at a local deli. I beg her to pick a vegetarian option, just for today, and she obliges without asking me why. I think if I see her consume any more of that vile color I'll surely be sick. I can't handle it. Not in this state.

We return to my studio, and I collapse. The stained tarps reek of iron and sweat and sex, but I couldn't care less. In fact, I roll in it. I allow whatever leftovers to stain my clothes and skin. I bury my face in the saturated center and will myself not to shout.

"What happened?" Zahra asks.

I don't reply. I gag, choking on the wallowing, my self-pity and anger. I'm pathetic, despicable, all the adjectives for *miserably misunderstood* and *mistreated with inequity*. Typically I'd be embarrassed, but I find myself unable to express anything else.

Zahra seems to grow a bit panicked by this, pacing about the room, searching for a solution. "You know what you need?" she says. "You need some airflow in here. That's what you need."

A squeak bursts out of me. I lift my head to shout *No!* but it's too late. Zahra's slim finger flips the switch. The fan jolts to life with a determined *whir*.

I cover the back of my neck, the tender spot that holds my brain stem, and brace myself as razor-sharp blades come crashing down. I can hear them *plink* one after the other, five in total, one for each blade of the fan, until all is silent.

Thankfully none of them hit me, and I look up to see if the same fate befell Zahra. She is unscathed, standing there delirious, and I realize that should she have been hit, it would not have mattered.

Zahra approaches one of the blades, bends, and picks it up. She turns it over. It glints in the studio light, and her color grows. I watch her face curdle. I watch her run her thumb down the serrated edge. She bleeds, and I watch her allow thick droplets of her color to drip onto my floor.

She looks at me. "This is what you use to . . ."

She is not sure how to say it, so I finish the thought for her. "To kill? Yes."

"How many?"

"What do you mean?"

"How many of them before me?"

Before her? What a funny frame of thought. Before her—I don't believe anything could exist before her. There is just her, the start of her, and the silly, trivial things that occurred in another life. Another timeline wholly separate from now. This is the sole spectrum in which we alone can live. Everything else is monochromatic.

But she wants an answer.

"Ten," I say.

"So that would make me the eleventh?"

I laugh. "If that's how you wish to think about it."

"Were they better than me?"

Suddenly it hurts to be amused. To find humor in the face of such an idiotic question.

Were they better than her?

"They do not even come close to what you are." And then, as

if evidence will prove my point: "Do you wish to see them?"

She presses her lips together, steps forward, but hesitates, like she's worried she might get bruised from approaching too fast, too quickly. Silently, she nods.

I stand and gather a large sketchpad from a corner of my studio. I beckon her, and together we sit on the floor.

"You've painted them?" she asks.

I shake my head. "No. I've painted *with* them."

I flip through the sketchpad, each page a sample of what I have taken from each number. A first draft of the exhibitions they inspired. Ten samples in total, the old intermingled with the new to test how well they'd cooperate, if their cross-pollination would create something marvelous. For the most part the experiments were a success. But compared to Zahra, these colors are lesser, diluted, and airy.

"Why would you paint with them?" she asks.

I allow her to take the sketchpad from my hands, and I look up at my ceiling as if there I might collect my thoughts.

I explain to her what I see. The color that surrounds every individual, a hue some might call an aura but I think of as another spectrum of energy, a light I alone have the correct cones and rods for. How people sense it at their core when I hide it in my paintings but just can't see it the way I can. I explain the existence of her color, how unique and indescribable it is. She asks me to try to describe it, and I tell her the human language fails where she begins.

"What's your color?" she asks.

I frown. "I do not have one."

Her eyes lift, hover over my head like she might be able to see something there. Instead, she mirrors my expression. "Oh."

"Zahra, I need you to do something for me."

I stand and face her, towering over her. I need her to willingly agree, to want this just as much as I do. There is no other way. I cannot confine her with death. She is truly free of my control. So I need her to agree. She looks up at me, lips parted, but does not move.

"I need you to stay with me," I tell her. "At least for a little while. However long you please, but at least for a little while. Will you do that? Will you do that for me?"

She looks unconvinced, suspicious. There's a moment where the particles between us charge and I can tell she sees clearer. I can tell she understands what I'm asking of her, that I truly do need her. A bleeding muse.

"What did the gallery owner say to you?" she asks.

I clench my jaw, teeth clacking. But it's only fair she knows.

"She thinks my art has gone tired," I say, and leave it at that.

Zahra nods like she knew this already, and maybe she did. She just needed the confirmation, the words out of my own mouth.

"I'll make you a deal." She holds up the sketchpad, open to a page with not just a sample of one color or two but the collective. Multiple colors fighting for space on a claustrophobic field. "There can be no others. I'll give you what you want, but I want no others. I want it to be just you and me. I want you to be happy with only me."

I find it in me to laugh. There could be no others. Not ever again. Not before her, not after her.

"Yes," I say. "Yes, of course. You have your deal."

She bites her bottom lip, contemplating. But I know what she'll say. We both know each other's darkness now. We are the only two beings on this earth, its heavens and hells, who can harmlessly feed into the other. A snake eating its own tail, forever hungry yet forever providing. She wants this as much as I do. She needs this.

"Yes," she says. "If it will make you happy, then yes."

THE COLOR OF BLOOD

MONA KABBANI

METACHROMATIC

The first night is a touch awkward. Zahra complains I have no food, which really means I have no meat. I tell her she can order grocery delivery for whatever she desires, and when the bill hits my account and the bags arrive, I help her transfer everything into my fridge. The sight of it all causes me to nearly vomit. My fridge is now a home for the most atrocious color in all of existence. There is one package tucked between a layer of ground beef and deli slices that glows a sunny yellow. This perplexes me until I decide I will not be eating it anyway so I should not care.

I stand in the center of my studio, spotlight on me, fan turned on above my head because Zahra says the airflow in here is nonexistent. She stands just behind me, running her fingers up and down my back. I've never had imposter syndrome before, and I'm not sure I have it now, but I do have it for my subject. For the phoenix I've insisted on portraying.

Does it have much to offer? Does it have *anything* to offer, besides glowing feathers and an age-old legend?

How does that legend go again?

The phoenix lives for centuries, for five hundred years, but only one may live at a time.

Zahra's fingertips slip into the waistband of my sweatpants. She tickles at my muscles, her touch traveling around my hips to my front.

The phoenix lives, and when it decides to live no longer, whether from boredom or loneliness, it lights itself on fire. For a moment it becomes the sun. It destroys itself. It dies to allow a new one to live in its place. To rise from the ashes.

Hands curl around my thigh. The undersides of Zahra's knuckles press into me in succession.

I nudge her off. I tell her I'm trying to concentrate. She whines.

"What do you think of when you see this?" I ask.

She eyes the canvas and clicks her tongue. "A bird."

"That's it?"

"A very pretty bird."

I turn to face her. She stares at me, grinning. I grab her by the shoulders and push her down onto the tarps I have still not yet replaced. I pull down my sweatpants so the band is around my ankles. I lift the dress she is wearing and use my knees against the back of her thighs to spread her legs apart. She moans as I slide inside her. Her color pulses and I dig my hands into it, wrapping my fingers around her neck. She frowns, her eyebrows coming together in a V. She shakes her head and gestures to the canvas, to the palette knife glowing a soft orange laid out on the easel.

I release her neck and say, "That knife is made out of bone, do you understand? From one of the ten."

She scrunches her nose, thinks, then decides she's okay with it. It's for her pleasure, after all.

I grab the palette knife from the easel and return to my previous position, easing myself inside of her again. I ask her where she wants it. She says "Surprise me," so I drive it into her chest as I thrust, feeling her ribs *crack* to make way for the blade. Color bubbles in the cradle of her cleavage. It saturates her green dress, and I make a mental note to order her a closet of clothing. She moans; I thrust harder. Suddenly she is silent, and I think she has climaxed, but I am too busy in my thoughts. I'm thinking about that bird. About fire and feather.

She taps out when she's done with me and I roll over, removing the blade, only to find that a part of it has snapped off. I tear her dress in half, exposing her chest, but the wound has already healed up. Accessibility to the shard of bone now lodged within her chest cavity, gone.

We look at each other.

She shrugs. "It's probably fine."

"I have more palette knives."

"That's good."

I ask her to stay exactly the way she is. I grab a paintbrush from my easel and spend some time back and forth between the canvas and her chest. When I am done, when her color has dried to the point of uselessness, I tell her to stand.

We both look at the painting.

"Now what do you see?" I ask.

"Still just a bird. Only now it bleeds."

~

We can't seem to fall asleep on anything except the vinyl tarps. Like our bodies are magnetized to the center of my studio, nervous and shaky when too far away. We've tried my bed. We've tried taking walks on the rooftop. I've shown her the tub I use to dissolve the bodies I will never again take. I show her the incinerator. She asks what I think would happen if we put her in there. Would she heal? Or would the flames be too much? Would they consume her until there is nothing left but ash?

I tell her I don't want to find out.

I show her the views of the city, point to the various buildings, and recite interesting facts about their architecture. She feigns interest. When we get too close to the edge of the rooftop, her skin pales, and she takes a quick step back as though her bravery is suddenly consumed by an immense amalgamation of fear.

The rooftop is clearly not her favorite place. She doesn't like the bed and can barely stand to be in my kitchen for longer than it takes to cook a meal. So we lay on the tarps. We hold each other—

barely, the flat surface unforgiving toward our embrace, but we try.

I think about the boardwalk. How Zahra looked up at the Ferris wheel in horror. Her avoidance of anything reaching a height greater than a couple of stories. Her feet always on the ground.

"You're afraid of heights," I say, less of a question and more of a realization. My arm strains beneath her ribcage, pinned between her heartbeat and the floor.

"I guess you could say that," she says. "I don't particularly like them. I can stomach them."

Her fingers graze the indentations of my bicep, lift, and then return to the curves of my cheeks.

"Why would a girl who cannot die be afraid of heights?"

She is silent for a moment. When she speaks, her voice is deep, a hole bottomed with pain.

"I broke my body against the earth once. Broke every single bone. Split my skin open, and I'm thankful my insides didn't spill out. It took three days to put myself back together. Three excruciating days to heal."

Her nails trace my lips, the bridge of my nose, the soft skin of my lower lid.

"How did that happen?" I ask.

Her oil-slick eyes gaze at me with intense warmth.

"I was climbing for the sun," she says. "I learned to mountain climb just for that reason. Because I think I am the only person on this earth who looks directly at the sun and feels not pain but pleasure. So I climbed in the hopes that I would get closer.

Because I thought we were destined to be together, the sun and me. Maybe I could reach it, maybe I could hold my hand out and cradle its boiling edge in the cup of my palm and I'd heal. I'd touch it and heal, and the sun would experience human contact for the first time and be so happy." She chuckles. "But my foot slipped. And I fell. And I had to heal at the base of that mountain instead."

I open my mouth to formulate more questions: *Why would you attempt something so silly? How could you think you'd ever touch the sun? How much did it hurt? Were you scared?*

She silences me with her fingertips in my eyes, pads stroking my corneas gently, oh, so very gently. There's a nip, a slight pressure, then relief as she pulls out my brown contacts, leaving me exposed.

"These have to hurt, don't they?" she asks, pinching the two together between her thumb and index finger and dangling them in the air like aged carcasses.

"Yes, they do."

"Why do you wear them?"

She runs her palm over my smooth scalp, drags her touch down to my hairless chest like she's painting me in strokes.

I'm not sure how to answer.

I don't want to make people uncomfortable. I don't want to scare them away. I want them to accept me. To love me. I want to lurk amongst them, truth hidden.

I want to be seen as an artist, not a monster.

Zahra smiles, grins. She rolls over onto her back, her spine crushing my wrist. Her chin lifts toward the ceiling, neck at an arch so the length of her throat pierces the air. I watch her mouth widen until it's a shape far too big for her face. Her tongue rolls out. She lifts her hand, fingertips like a crane, and releases.

My contacts fall into her mouth. She swishes her tongue within her cheeks this way and that. She swallows.

What an appetite, I think. *My palette knife, my eyes, inside of her.*

And then I wonder what else is inside of her.

She laughs. She laughs and it's a graveyard of echoes. Of items she has taken into her hands and eaten. And when she rolls over to kiss me, I feel the energy of all that's within her. I feel the synthetic sight from my consumed contact lenses, the bone of whichever number I killed to create the blade of that palette knife. Those echoes travel through infinity, through Zahra's throat and soul, just to break open the back of my skull and see if I'd heal.

~

"Have you always seen color?"

I've set up a series of blank canvases in a semicircle around the studio. I'm working on one now, outlining its detail with exquisite precision.

"What was that?"

"I asked if you've always seen color," Zahra repeats.

"Oh." I exhale and pull back from my painting. I have to remove myself from my art to think, which is funny. You'd think art is what makes me think. "I have."

"Have you always been so homicidal about it?"

I glare at her, then shake my head. "No, I have not. The"—I smirk—"*homicidal* tendencies didn't come until I started developing my art."

"When was that?"

"When was what?"

"Your first kill."

"Oh, it was so long ago," I tell her. "But I remember enough. At least, I remember until I don't."

I was in college. I was taking a course on the theory of color and the subconscious. There was a boy in my class, a first year, like me. He sat down next to me on day one. Simply plopped his wiry frame a foot from mine despite the lecture hall being expansive and nearly empty. He had golden hair, fluffy, and he used to comment on how my hair was somehow more golden than his. How my eyes were like crystals while his were a weak blue.

His color was another I cannot describe. Something I've seen variations of since but nothing quite the same. The color I can most closely relate it to for those who cannot see is an emerald green. It was breathtaking.

We were as close as I could comfortably get. Our relationship was difficult because I couldn't get the thought of my lie being exposed out of my head. I struggled with intimacy. I was close and then I was distant, and it broke his heart. He thought there was something wrong with him, and I could never tell him that the problem was me. That I was hiding something terrible in plain sight.

I dreaded him seeing me. Catching me off guard or sensing my strangeness, the corruption that was my body and soul. Every day I woke up terrified with a pit the size of a fist lodged in my chest, swallowing all hope—a vacuum designed to vaporize any dream of our future together, leaving only thoughts of eventual immolation.

One day we were in my room. He was in my bed under the covers, shivering because the heaters in the dorm rooms had gone out and it was midwinter. He just looked so inviting. I wanted to help him get warm. I wanted my bodily contact to bring him some form of comfort.

I slid into bed with him, and he wrapped his arm around my waist. He drew me in closer and I did not object. I ran my fingers through his hair and felt how different the texture was to my own—human, where mine was synthetic. It was like dipping my hands into a vat of liquid gold. Everything about him was wonderful: soft where I was rough, curved where I was sharp. I wanted to touch him forever.

He mimicked my movements, and I did not realize my mistake, my careless negligence, until he pulled my hair. For whatever reason—perhaps flirtatious playfulness or sexual foreplay—he simply grabbed a fistful of my hair and yanked.

Alas, the spark I had been dreading. The ember to commence the fire that would destroy us both.

My wig came off. He screamed. It was awful and shrill. Pervasive and obliterating. The sound wrenches me from my dreams in a cold sweat even now.

And the look of sheer horror etched across his beautiful face . . . his eyes, dilated and wide, volleyed into survival mode in the face of such savagery, gaping at *me*.

I wanted that terror to stop. To please, *god*, just *stop*.

Some people say they see red when they go into fits of rage, but all I saw was his color. An overwhelming saturation of it. I reached for that color, grabbed it, held on to it for dear life, and did not let go. When my vision cleared, I had his broken neck in my hands.

"You killed him?" Zahra says, bewildered.

"You asked me about my first."

She frowns. "But you loved him."

I think about this and nod. In my own way and in his own way, yes, she is correct. I loved him and he loved me.

"What was his name?"

"I don't remember . . . just that he was number one."

A lie.

His name was Alexander.

~

"I think it's kind of romantic," Zahra says.

The rays from the sun penetrate my studio. They reflect off Zahra's skin, accentuating the deeper tones in her flesh, like fresh-pressed olive oil rippling beneath the surface. Where the sun does her divine justice, it beats down upon me, drawing a sweat. I run my sleeve across my forehead before the limpid beads of salt drip into my eyes, temporarily blinding me.

"What is?" I ask, guiding the fortified sable hair of my paintbrush across my canvas in the elegant bends of an arabesque. I'm maintaining Zahra in my periphery as reference, noting her metronomic stride as she approaches.

"This kind of selection of color. How you spot a person in the street and it's almost like love at first sight."

"Hmm." I dip my brush into the rinse cup, choose a new color, then drag the bristles beside a feather, darkening the space around it to inversely paint the illusion of light. "But I do not love them."

"Sure, you do." Zahra sets the glass of water I'd requested on the tripod table. "It's just a different kind of love."

I stop painting, step back, and look at her. "Can you love something you're only intent on killing?"

She shakes her head, a delicate curl forming on the corner of her mouth. As she speaks, it expands into awe. "I don't think you look at it that way. I think you immortalize them. I think the way *you* think about it is that you're turning them into something greater than they could ever be alive."

"Yes," I agree. "I suppose you could say that for some."

Straining a grin in her direction, I reach for the glass of water and take three deep gulps to quench my building thirst. It isn't until the fourth gulp when I witness Zahra's awe turn into revolted horror that I taste the metallic grease glazing my tongue, chemically perfumed and foul.

"Void . . ." Zahra says, reaching for me like her hand will be the anchor that saves me from the roiling sea.

I do not respond. I spit what remains in my mouth—a thick coating of turpentine and pigment—back into the container, lower the cup, and gape at the taupe liquid buoying thick clumps of oily color I have just swallowed down like cereal.

I look at the tripod table. At the paints and brushes and stained rags that clutter its surface, turning it into a Rorschach of an artist's delirium. At the glass of water I was supposed to drink that was placed right beside the dirty rinse cup I now hold in my hand.

I look at Zahra. Guilt curdles her face.

"Void—" she attempts again, but I have felt the pressure in my system drop, my temperature plummet, and I am already rushing to the bathroom, ignoring her calls.

I'm on my knees when the nausea spews forth, landing in my toilet bowl. A collection of colors brilliant and hideous—ironically the only time *color* has ever come from my being. Zahra is behind me upon my third retch, and after I have dry-heaved all that my diaphragm will allow, she hands me the cup of water I was meant to drink.

"It's like you just swallowed a vial of poison," she comments.

I rest my spine against the bathtub, catching my breath, then chug the water to remove the taste of vomit and fumes from my throat. "In effect, I did. Oil-based paints are toxic. They can be lethal if ingested in large quantities."

And I am not like you, I think after setting the empty glass on the tiled floor. *I cannot take risks with my life.*

She nods, then grows quiet.

With this cold tile beneath us and these introspective

comparisons floating in the air—should Zahra have drunk the rinse cup in its entirety, nothing would have happened—we fidget uncomfortably. I want for this silence that punctuates my mortality to end. I want to remind her that I am still very much alive.

"I think you were a bit too overconfident before, by the way," I tell her.

"Oh?" She perks up at this. "About what?"

"About me and my motives for killing." I rub my tongue against my palate to clear out the lingering flavors, then say, "I killed my first mentor, I'll have you know. And that is one you would agree was not motivated by love."

Zahra takes a seat on the floor in front of me. She weaves her legs through mine so that we are a pretzel, two pieces baked into one. "What happened?"

I shrug, playing off my emotions as though they do not exist. "He was a talentless pervert. A user where I once thought I saw greatness." I do not tell her of his coarse hands. How they pitter-pattered across my skin like wet gravel on silk. "He had a color like rotten wildberries mixed with concentrated piss, and at first I thought it was a testament to his defiance. The bold indifference he communicated to the world around him and the fearlessness he displayed in his artistic exploits." I click my tongue, then flick my wrist as if to remove something viscid from my fingertips. "He had a studio very much like my own, only he did not live in his as I do. He kept his work and home life compulsively separate. I did not mind. I had no interest in meeting his wife and his kids. A long day's work to then be invited over for a quaint family dinner? No. I only wanted to sit and look at his art. He loved to watch me look.

"One day we were in his studio. It had been a year of stalling. A year of pathetic sketches and uninspired palettes. His art, I'd come to realize, was merely composite copies of other great works stitched together with cheap paint. The rose-colored lenses melted and I saw him for what he was." I press my lips together, and I can taste the air from that day: metallic; bitter. "He had this paperweight he loved so much," I recall. "It was made of precious quartz found on some far-off island. I used it to break his skull before he could waste any more of my time." I gesture toward the studio outside of the bathroom, blowing air between my lips. "I stored samples of his color somewhere in my sketchbooks but never used it for my own art. I wanted to destroy everything that existed of him."

Zahra places her warm palm on my knee and I flinch, breathing out of the memory. She smiles meekly but does not remove her touch.

"What was his name?" she asks.

I shake my head. "It does not matter. I burned it to cinder along with his body a long time ago. In fact, he was the first I burned!"

I laugh suddenly, thinking about how Alexander's and my mentor's aftercare were so vastly different. I buried Alexander six feet under the cold, forest ground before winter's first snowfall; I burned my faux mentor's body in a trashcan fire in the middle of the night, then hid what remained throughout the city for the rats to eat.

"Hate," Zahra says, tasting the flavor of the word. "So caustic." She crawls onto my lap, curling her body around the base of my torso, and I hold her in my arms as she strokes the underside of my jaw, this divine beauty in human skin. "Do you think you could ever hate me like that?"

"You?" I chuckle. "I don't think I'm capable of it. No. Not when it's you."

~

Zahra can't seem to understand that no means no. She has complained that I am not putting her to good use. That I am tiptoeing around an artistic adventure, and my excuse of "planning" is getting lame.

"I think you're just scared," she says.

"I have to make sure I get it right."

"A scared, scared man."

"I can't mess this up! There's too much at stake."

"It's the zebra all over again."

I peer over my canvas at her. My blood starts to heat—a delicate, low simmer.

"What did you say?"

"I said, it's the zebra thing all over again. You're scared of your own art. Of any abandonment of what you know. Of color. Of an exploration of something else. It's pathetic, really."

My nostrils flare. I clench my fist, paintbrush in hand. The wood of the handle weeps beneath the pressure. I think about

Number Ten, how I tore her open. How I let her spill out onto my canvas without a care. How the impact amazed me.

"I'm not afraid," I insist. "I'm calculated."

"Same thing. The gallery owner is getting inside your head. Your fear of failure is what will *make* you fail. I'm here, waiting for you. Waiting for you to just fucking *man up* and actually create something!"

The paintbrush snaps in my fist. I round the easel, grab Zahra by the hair at the nape of her neck, and drive the jagged end of the paintbrush into the space between her collarbones. She smiles. She smiles the entire time I dig into her, carving a line up to the underside of her jaw, splitting her throat open, watching the flesh and cartilage part like the sea. She bleeds heavily and she smiles.

"Fih-nuh-uhlly," she croaks through her broken trachea.

For a moment, I wonder if I am even doing this. If I am even here right now in my studio, her body pressed up against mine, her color flowing down our chests to our feet. I wonder if she's dead. If I'm waltzing with a corpse. If I've finally killed her.

But she's leaning in to kiss my neck, pressing her body closer to mine so I can feel her heat.

I trust her. I trust that she is here.

When she pulls away, I return the favor, kissing the spot where her wound has already healed. My heart rate accelerates to meet with the pulsing of her throat, and I find myself growing hard, an idea blooming in my mind. I step back, kick at the easels so they fall, spilling the canvases across the floor. I arrange the frames faceup, in sporadic order. I lie down, my body across them, and let Zahra strip me as I accommodate by shifting around for her. She hikes up her skirt and straddles my waist.

Jackson Pollock's easel was the floor, the earth. He wasn't afraid of it. He was in love with gravity. He spilled paint every which way. He stained everything he ever worked on—so much so that his wife had to cover their barn floor with marble to forget about him.

I hope I am not forgotten. I hope my art bleeds through these tarps and stains my floors. I hope Zahra's color becomes a permanent installation. I hope I bleed into her and she into me. I hope we can combine to create something cataclysmic.

As she rocks, I place the broken paintbrush in her hand. She takes it and I nod in encouragement, tapping my index finger to my bare chest.

I want permanent proof. I want to feel it. I want our existence to have evidence. A love story painted in scars.

When the paintbrush enters me, I experience a strange dissociation. I see the gore, the act of my skin being torn apart, flesh unfurling like a flower of thick petals, but I do not feel it. I bleed and the color is as blood should be. Cherry red and hot. She drags the jagged end over a centimeter, my skin protesting the damage, and that's when the pain comes. The sting sparkles across my skin like I've set off fireworks atop my chest—*bang!*—snaps exploding in an ombré, some kind of gradient from the heart of the wound until the pain fades out around my shoulders. I howl, and she drags the paintbrush down a centimeter more before pulling it out and howling too.

I grab her. I flip her beneath me. I will my exposed insides to bleed against her chest, her neck, her smile. I thrust into her so hard we shift back a foot. We readjust. We roll to the left, to the right. She regrips the paintbrush and drives it into my hip, just above the bone. I scream and I laugh and with each thrust the exhilaration digs deeper inside of me. The pain is iron and velour. It's pure, untainted euphoria.

The wound in her neck has since healed, but I don't want to be forgotten. I don't want her to stare at her body naked in the mirror and recognize no trace of me. No memory of me on her skin.

I lean down. I wrap my teeth around the soft flesh above her right breast. I tense; I bite. She cries out in ecstasy, and I'm surprised by how easily the flesh tears away. How this lump of what I assume is dead or dying skin was a part of her and now is fully detached and inside of me. Her color pools in the wound. Dribbles down the edges like tears. I think about swallowing as I roll her flesh around my tongue, soft like velvet yet substantial like a salted stone from the bottom of a warm lake. I think about the tip of my palette knife broken off inside of her, floating in the expanse of her organ tissue. She looks so beautiful beneath me. So radiant and ethereal as she's pushed back and forth, over and around.

An animalistic craving overcomes me.

I want her taste to remain with me forever.

I swallow and relish as she slides down my throat, nestles comfortably within my stomach. She squeaks and I dip my lips into the hole in her chest limned with my teeth marks: a perfect dental portrait were her body ever to be found. I kiss the wet canvas beneath. Kiss her shoulders and arms. Thrust faster, harder, lap at her. She moans, she screams. She starts to cry, but they're sobs of joy, an overwhelming pleasure so vicious it's breaking the nerves in her body. Snapping them like brittle twigs. I bet beneath it all, those nerves are lighting up like the northern sky. Reaching the peak of their illumination before dying off one by one.

The wound above her breast starts to shut, new skin pushing out the pool of color. I flip her over before I can see it, my erasure on the collage that is her body. I'll never be permanent. I'll never be a part of her, to love and to mark for all of eternity.

I rip the paintbrush out of her hands. I ram it into her back, into the muscle beside her spine. I pull it out and an arc of color follows. I drive it into her again. Again and again and again until her back is a ruinous field of craters. Her screams pierce my ears. I think she's come to a climax because everything is so much sleeker. So wet. Or perhaps it's the color she bleeds filling out this room. Rising and rising until it drowns us both.

My fingers are in her back, pulling out skin. Digging canyons and graves in which I might be able to bury my existence. I'm begging. I'm pleading. I can feel myself crying, which is so bizarre. I'm trying to swallow my emotions. My romantically disheveled brain is so confused by this pain. I've climaxed inside of her and barely even noticed. But I feel the aftershock. The hurricanes and earthquakes emanating from beneath.

The wounds on her back stitch themselves together. They push my fingers out. Heal, seal. Her color radiates. A single pulse of it knocks me off balance and I feel myself losing consciousness. My foot slips. I'm falling against her spine.

If only one of those graves had stayed open long enough for me to fall into.

~

The gallery owner has called to ask where I've been. She has emailed several times demanding a response. It's been weeks, she says. She's starting to get worried.

I lie across the chairs of my kitchen island at an obtuse angle. Zahra, in nothing but a bra and panties so as not to stain her clothes, hovers above me with a curved needle in hand as I type, delete, and retype my email response.

Concern is entirely unnecessary, I write. *You asked and I shall deliver.*

"Ow, *fuck*," I hiss when the needle pokes through a particularly tender spot in the flayed surface wound just below my ribs.

"Sorry, sorry!" Zahra chirps.

She has no idea what she's doing, her medical degree a curriculum of YouTube videos and online articles. But she's spent hours, days, researching after I nearly bled out from a burst wound, platelets nowhere to be found. Bandages and gauze were no longer doing the trick and as much as Zahra enjoys playing the artist, painting the contours of my body with the fresh blood from my wounds, I cannot bleed like she does.

When she is done stitching me back together, she stands tall and scans over her work: the series of scars, some more healed than others; the cinched-up wounds she's recently worked on, leading to fresh craters of body heat and biological hell.

"I think I'm getting better," she comments.

I nod and tell her that I think she is, too, but she needs to be more careful about where she's sticking that needle.

"Just be thankful you're not dead . . . or infected," she says. "What can I do to make you happy? Would you like something for breakfast?"

She steps up to the stove and reaches for a pan hanging from a series of hooks nailed to the wall.

I mumble something about still being a vegetarian and return to my computer. My pinky taps the ENTER key, and when the little icon of an envelope seals shut and disappears into the fiber-optic ether, I hear the clatter of metal hitting the floor. It's so sudden and grating it nearly blinds me so that when I look up, I'm not sure what I'm seeing—or rather, what I'm not seeing.

Zahra, there moments ago stretched above the stove to reach for a pan, is curled into herself. Her pronounced spine, the jutting vertebrae leading into the back of her bra strap, is the only part of her visible just above the kitchen island countertop.

"Zahra?"

She heaves—the sound of an animal losing all sense of respiratory function—and I bolt upright from my seat. I barely register my laptop falling from my lap, the corner cracking against the floor, pieces of plastic breaking off and creating music like a rattlesnake's tail.

"Zahra," I repeat, less of a question now and more of a plea for her to answer me.

I'm at her side and I grab her before she collapses to the floor. She's convulsing, her body lurching in a ripple effect from stomach to head like she's trying to push something out.

"Come," I say, "come, come, come, come, come." I'm whispering aggressively under my breath, hoping the command will marionette her body to my will. "Come, come, come."

I lead her toward the bedroom. She digs her heels in, stopping us both, and shakes her head. The tarps it is. I lay her down. She's in a fetal position. I ask her what's wrong, to tell me where it hurts. She shakes her head like her refusal will rid her of the pain. Like being defiant will help either of us.

"Zahra . . . Zahra, please."

Are there tears in my eyes? I'm stressed and panicked and can taste her suffering like barbed wire brushed across my tongue. I grab her wrists and hold them both in my one hand despite her struggling against me. I pin them above her head while trying to pin her thighs to the ground with my knees. She writhes and bucks, but I manage. Just enough to see.

About three inches below her sternum is a bulge. An embossment in the shape of a blade. A jagged edge.

The broken remnant of my palette knife.

"Fuck!" I curse, and throw her limbs away from me in shock.

I stand, hands trembling, and watch her cloud of shifting color squirm, now finally reactive to the convulsing girl within it. I return to her, breaching that storm, and hold her against my chest, try to get a steady, comfortable grip on her so she stops moving. So she doesn't hurt herself or turn in a way that pierces the palette knife through something vital. Her lungs—her heart?

Will she die this time? Will this be what kills her?

"*Shh*, Zahra, *shh* . . .*"

I pet her hair, grease her roots with her own sweat. Inhale steadily and deeply. Exhale against her cheek in the hopes that she will feel my breathing, sense it within her core, and calm.

It works. Slowly, but it works.

She lies tense but still in the cave of chest and arms I have created out of my body for her. We breathe, and when I feel the elasticity between her serenity and chaos has thickened, I speak.

"We need to get it out."

She nods. "I know."

"Will it hurt?"

"The cutting has never hurt."

"But will *this* hurt?"

"I don't think I have the liberty to wonder."

I lower her onto the tarps again, careful with every degree in case something should pinch and she escalates into another inconsolable fit. When she is supine, I return to my kitchen and retrieve a butcher's knife, one that is sturdy and I know will not break.

She looks so weak now that I stand above her. So small and fragile. Like I could press the ball of my foot into her shoulder and she would break apart into the infinitesimal dust particles that created her in the first place.

I straddle her carefully.

She frowns. "I don't like you being delicate with me."

"I don't like you being in pain."

I dip the blade of the butcher's knife into her skin. It slides up her stomach as easily as if through clay and she doesn't even wince. Doesn't even give so much as a muscle twitch. Simply stares up at the ceiling with complete indifference, jaws clenched, waiting. Simply waiting.

The blade hits the offending lump, slices over it. I think I can see the palette knife tucked within her severed flesh. I set the butcher's knife down and prod at the bloody slice, wiping away color, angling myself this way and that to see.

Ah, there it is! There's that stray fucker.

I reach inside of her, my fingertips disappearing between her folds of skin. I expect to find muscle fibers, blood, maybe an organ I'd push aside if I must slide in deep enough, but I don't.

I find an image instead. An illusion.

Not a body composed of parts, but a dream. A cataclysmic vision.

An event horizon.

~

When Jackson Pollock first discovered the sun, he used synthetic lightning to paint impossible shapes up and down his colossal tapestries. He foresaw the irrepressible power in the rings of Saturn and painted circles over and over and over and over and over and—

He invited the galaxies into the threads of his canvases and begged them to throw up on his curtains.

"That's the price of art," he said as the planets hosted a tea party within the bent wreckage of his automobile.

That's the price of art.

No, that's not right. But that's what the snails are telling me. The snails that live inside this place, their tails creating infinite loops. Spirals within spirals looping around a burning sun, everything here inverted, everything magnetic.

I'm falling out of reality. I've slipped and I'm falling and falling, and I'll break my body against the earth and I'll wonder . . . my *god* . . . how could I have ever thought myself to have any worth, my life any meaning, when the celestial gods open their mouths and don't even notice they've accidentally inhaled me too?

No, not celestial gods. Just one.

Zahra.

It's her. It was never me.

Oh god, oh *fuck*. I can tell by the way her insides, these snails, and this infinitely pressurized space work around my bones. Organs made of a thousand gray loops lapping at my very existence like I'm an ice cream cone. Like I'm a boring, lame ice cream cone held in the hands of a blond child larger than life who could not care less if a seagull came and swept me away.

And the void. It's nothing. I thought the absence of everything was the truth of the soul. But it's nothing. It's *fucking nothing*.

How arrogant. How stupid. How silly silly silly silly *silly silly*

silly of me.

I'm inside a god. And this god is filled with *everything*. I'm searching and searching. I need to get out. I need to be free of this. Why did I come here in the first place?

Something that does not belong hits my hand like my palm is a vacuum, and how dare it exist here. How dare I try to put something of myself in this supreme place.

I wrap my fingers around the object, and now that I've done their bidding, the snails eject me with their tails. I fly backward through shifting murk, color so vibrant yet dark at the same time, through the sun and planets and stars and constellations and open mouths of laughter that are laughing at me, they're *laughing at me*, asking *How could you be so dumb?*

~

I'm on the tarps, on my hands and knees, heaving. Zahra is alert, her arms around me. She's already sealed up, the worlds within her closed off to me, unwanting of me. The palette knife is below me, glowing with her color, its very nature transformed from its time living inside of her.

I whisper so harshly it strains my throat, *"Did you know?"*

"Did I know what? What are you talking about?"

She is frantic, patting down my back like she might find what's hurting me and remove it from my person.

Did you know what's inside of you? Did you know that there are entire worlds inside of you? The snails, the snails, oh god, the snails.

I want to ask, but I don't. I don't because to speak it into existence, into my studio that is my own slice of a kingdom, would be too much. And I'm still trying to comprehend. To wrap my brain around what I just experienced. How I reached inside of her and discovered something so horrifying, so ancient and eldritch. Something I could never have the mind to create.

I look up at Zahra, at her worried, pleading face.

I weep.

Oh, Zahra . . .

I weep.

~

In the coming days, Zahra's appetite is beyond the mere need to satiate. She's on top of me before I can put my paintbrush down. I reciprocate, but absent-mindedly, my thoughts elsewhere. Anywhere far, far away.

When I look at her, all I see is an unattainable infinity. I see the things I thought I was—transformative, revolutionary, divine—but can never be. Not in the ways she is. In the ways she is so effortlessly clueless to.

What's inside of me? I wonder. If she reached her hands into my body, would she find something just as remarkable, if not more? Do I possess something greater than her?

Oh, god.

I can never know. I do not heal. Not as she does. It is

impossible to test, to ask Zahra to slip her thin fingers inside of me and tell me what she finds. I'd be dead. And if in my last dying moments she tells me all she can feel is a slowing heartbeat, I'll die devastated.

It passes my mind briefly if I could do something with the worlds inside of her. If I could conquer them. If I could paint what I've seen, the emotions I felt, portray her for all to see in two dimensions. Put it to canvas, laugh, and say, *Ha! Now that I look at it, it's nothing impressive at all. It's absolutely nothing at all!*

But the thought of returning to that place to remember it in totality sends chills down my spine. Nauseates me. And I can't stop thinking about those snails inside of her. The ones I now recall would shrivel up, die, and be reborn over and over and over again under a blazing sun.

THE COLOR OF BLOOD

MONA KABBANI

MONOCHROMATIC

The gallery owner has waited long enough. This is what she expresses in a very stern email sent at six in the morning after I ignored fourteen of her calls.

The collection is done. Each frame filled, saturated, dripping with abstract gore. I can't stop them from dripping. It's Zahra's color. It never ends, as if the white of my canvases is bone marrow and the art hemopoiesis. Her color has taken on its own form, its own interpretation, its own continuous transfiguration.

The collection is complete because there is nothing more for me to do. The artist has been rendered useless.

Zahra tiptoes into my room, approaches my bed, asks why I don't sleep on the vinyl tarps with her. She tries to sit next to me, to touch my skin, and I flinch, cowering under her hovering hand. That hand that contains incomprehensible infinities, divine blood. When she hesitates, I take the opportunity to scooch myself away from her, clear my throat, regain my composure.

"I can't just sit here anymore. I have to show the gallery owner what I've created. The deadline is up."

Zahra, pursing her lips, digs her nails into her fingers, and I want to beg her to stop. Plead that she does not split herself open so I have to see what's inside of her again. I don't think I could handle it.

Instead, her skin stays intact, and she asks, "Are you happy?"

I look at her, this being who is greater than anything I could ever wish to achieve. Greater simply by existing.

I say with a smile, "I need you to leave."

"Is something wrong?"

"No. But I need to invite the gallery owner over. I need to show her what I've done. What her money and time has gone toward." *I need to hope, to get down on my knees and pray.* "I can't have you here when she critiques." *When she decides I'm a fraud.*

Zahra nods. She goes to place her hand on my thigh, stops when she sees me shrink away, then stands.

"I'll text you," she whispers.

I pretend I do not hear. I am looking at my computer screen, drawing circles on my trackpad. Infinite circles that make my cursor loop and loop and loop like the tails of inverted snails. Snails that whisper awful things in my ear. Remind me that I am an imposter. An observer.

A worthless void.

There's a *click* in the living room. I look up but already know she is gone. I can tell by the way my studio has depressurized. The ringing in my ears has stopped.

The snails have ceased their whisperings.

~

The gallery owner stands in my doorway wearing sunglasses like the world outside of her gallery is too ugly for her precious eyes to bear. Her posture is that of a typical curator, one who believes her every word is of utmost importance. Which is funny, since I've recently realized everything is meaningless.

Her composure breaks the moment she steps inside my studio. Her feet stumble midstride, as though an invisible wall stands suddenly erect before her. She hunches her shoulders, shoves her sleeved forearm to her snout.

"Jesus H. Christ, Void. It smells like death in here."

I chuckle nervously, fiddling my fingers behind my back.

"Have you lived in this this whole time? Have you even showered?" She takes off her sunglasses, eyebrows angled like winter hillsides, leans into me, and sniffs. "*Blech!* You smell like sweat and rust and . . . and *carrion!*"

"What a lovely comparison" is all I can think to say. I gesture my hand to the center of my studio. "Now that the work is complete, I'll have the time to clean."

I'm hoping she won't stay long, and I'm sure she's hoping the same. I'm hoping she'll take another few steps inside, take one look at the first canvas, stare at me with disgust, and walk right back out my door. I'll never hear from her again. I'll burn everything I own in that incinerator. I'll sell the studio. Sell what pieces of mine I have left to whoever offers the highest bid while my name still has meaning. While I'm still a breath away from being blacklisted.

I'll move into the Ferris wheel. I'll ride it forever and ever and ever until those snails decide they're bored with me and leave me in peace.

"What the hell is this?"

I snap out of my daydream. I turn to the gallery owner, who is leaning in to get a closer look at one of my paintings. They're all one color. They all drip and bleed Zahra's color, a dash of my own blood here and there where hers didn't ultimately consume mine. They all depict a timeline of a single, abstract subject. A birth. A life. A death.

A resurrection.

I don't even bother to explain the work. I brace myself for the onslaught. The curses. The scolding for being a waste of space, a waste of time.

This is what you call art?

This is what you promised?

You're a hack.

A phony.

A liar.

The gallery owner turns away, her head bowed to the floor, hands on her thighs like she's about to vomit. Heavy breaths. Such heavy breaths. She then clears her throat and stands to face the canvases again, taking them all in this time. Taking a good, hard look.

"Is the drip part of the design?" she asks.

"I can't seem to get it to stop," I admit.

Her eyebrow lifts and then lowers, accepting this. Not caring enough to find out why. Cost-benefit and such. It drips? So it drips. She nods.

"Did you paint these in your blood?" she asks.

"No," I say defensively, partially a reflex, partially because it's true.

She swallows, puts back on her sunglasses, clicks her heels together like Dorothy wanting to go home. Another curt nod. "We'll say you did. We'll say it's your blood, the famous artist of chromatics who bleeds in one color for his work. 'Come one, come all to see the painter's true nature,' and such."

She turns to me with a smile larger than life stretched across her face, lips threatening to split her visage in half. Pearly white teeth hungry with greed. Eyes shielded, soul gone.

"You sneaky dog, you." She laughs. Taps me on the shoulder with her open palm. "You've done it, Void. You've done something ... *cataclysmic*. I'll have the movers pick them up tonight."

"Tonight?"

"Yes, Void. Tonight."

Her tone implies she does not want to argue. Her tone says she's getting sick of the stench, sick of being in here, and she just wants to leave. Wants to leave and have someone pick the money up for her. Stick *their* hands in the dirty work.

"Okay. Tonight," I confirm.

When she shuts the door behind her, I turn and marvel. I see what I have created in a new light, and a part of me inflates inside. The work I've bled for. The work I dug my fingernails through all manner of skin and veins, bone and flesh, to get to. *Me.* This was all me, for of course this couldn't have been the makings of someone else. *I* am the artist. I am the king—no, the *god*—amongst colors.

My phone vibrates.

Around and around and around and—

I seem to remember a spiral. Snails and a Ferris wheel. This color unlike anything I have ever seen before leaking forth from the open wounds of olive flesh.

A girl.

Oh, yeah. What was her name again?

My cell phone buzzes. I look at its screen and see three texts from a familiar name.

Hey.

Is it over?

How did it go?

~

By the time Zahra comes over the canvases are gone. The movers have come and cleared the space out. They complained about the drip, about the leak that seems to never end, and I told them they'll have to get plastic mats—thirty-gallon garbage bags, in fact—because their assumptions are correct.

The drip, although only that—a drip—does not stop.

Zahra glances around at the space, twirls in circles within the room that has been cleared of everything that was once a part of her. The stench is gone, the color wiped from the exposed floorboards, shelves, cabinets, anywhere else the blood spatter reached. Dried bits of flesh meticulously pried off whatever surface they once lived on.

She looks at me, wonder and awe in her oil-slick eyes. "So . . . I take it the gallery owner was pleased?"

I grin. I chuckle. I stifle a laugh. I grab her by the waist positioning us to waltz and spin her around this newly cleared room. Hold her face between my hands and kiss her frail little nose. Her pillowy lips. Her laughter echoes off these emptied walls.

I take her to a restaurant, where I order the most expensive items on the menu. Where I indulge in a bottle of red wine from the restaurant owner's personal collection. Sweet tobacco, Spanish cedar, dried flowers, dark mushrooms and roses. Another bottle? Of course! Why not? Surprise me. It's a celebration, after all. I toast to myself, to my success. Zahra, sitting across from me, toasts to my success. Her color undulates, shifts, highlights all the colors surrounding us in this dim, candlelit restaurant.

Blue, lust, green, disgust, intrigue, purple.

I could paint them all. I could create worlds with their entrails.

"Would you like to go to the boardwalk?" Zahra asks, leaning in, her eyes returning to my view. "You know, to round off the celebration?"

I pay the tab and add a thirty percent tip. I take the long way to the boardwalk. I don't want to see the gallery windows just yet. I don't want to see what my work looks like outside of my studio walls. Not yet.

Zahra wants to throw basketballs into oval hoops. Toss rings around the thick necks of glass soda jars. I want to look at the lights. At all the rides and their polka-dot colors. The Ferris wheel.

I want to go on the Ferris wheel.

I turn to Zahra, my hand wrapped around her waist, a smile on both of our faces, although hers looks so fake now. So conditional. I think about the Ferris wheel and how we'll never be able to go on it because she's afraid of heights. Afraid she might break her body on the earth and need three days to heal. I think about how I'll always be grounded, weighed down by her and her worries and her expectations and her fears.

I don't think I want you anymore, I say to no one. I repeat it in my mind over and over and over again like a chant.

I don't think I can do this anymore.

I think I'm done.

I don't think I want you anymore.

Zahra giggles. "Why are you looking at me like that? You look so intense." Her finger travels up my stomach, suggestively probing my muscles for an answer. "Is there something on your mind?"

I don't want you anymore.

"No, love. Nothing at all. Oh, did you already use up all your throws? And you didn't land a single one? Aw, such a shame. No more zebras in your future, then. Hmm? I see. Fine. Sir, how much is it for another throw?"

~

I leave the studio in the morning to pick up what has become our daily breakfast muffins. I've managed to convince Zahra to stop eating meat altogether. If she wants to live in my studio, I cannot bear the sight any longer. She's grown to really enjoy the taste of corn muffins.

It's a particularly sunny day. I'm wearing Ray-Bans with a gold trim, a black shirt, and black pants, so I make my walk brisk lest I melt into an obsidian puddle on the sidewalk. The speed doesn't help. After a few streets, I'm coated in a thin layer of sweat that is infinitely replenished as I use my shirt to dab here and there. I should have just ordered in. I thought the walk would be a nice escape. A nice moment of solitude.

I hurry my pace for another block, then stop in my tracks.

There's a familiar face in my periphery. Two, in fact.

I approach the graffitied newspaper box and open the small plastic window. A newspaper leaning against the door falls out, and I catch it before it hits the ground. It's the local post's latest edition, fresh off the press. The newspaper unfolds in my hands, releasing the scent of ink and sweet-almond musk, and I see the front-page image of me and Zahra on the boardwalk, hand in hand. She is smiling up at me with what I swear is a visible twinkle in her eye, and I, towering over her like a pale, moon-lit monolith, appear to be glaring directly at the camera, slightly hunched, body language so clearly uninviting, although I had no idea someone was taking our picture at the time.

The headline reads, *VOID'S MYSTERIOUS BEAU.*

The newspaper crinkles within my grip. I don't bother reading on. I empty the box of its contents, a stack the height of my chest, and throw every page into the nearest trashcan. I know there are other newspaper boxes in this city. I know there are other presses printing similar articles. I know my reaction is futile. But seeing our faces at the bottom of a bin makes me feel infinitely better. To own myself with this act of defiance.

Masking the twist of anger in my expression, I continue my walk, straightening my posture once or twice when I notice myself hunching over. I wince at the raw tissue held together by amateur stitches threatening to pop beneath my shirt, marring the space just below my shriveling heart. I could tear those wounds open right now and bleed my own warmth, relish in the sensation trickling down my chest for all to see on this city street, just to remind myself that I have free will. That I, too, bleed. But I don't.

Reaching my destination, I grab the diner's door handle, tug, and grunt when I am met with resistance. I lift my sunglasses to the top of my head, peer into the dark diner windows.

Shit. *Fuck.* The place is closed.

There's a rattle from the other side of the door, a *snap*, and the squeak of unoiled hinges. I am greeted by blond hair and long limbs. A nervous disposition. The color purple.

"Sorry, we open late on Mondays and Thursdays now."

The waiter. *This* waiter. I've seen him before. So, so long ago. What feels like ages now.

I would remember that color anywhere.

"Oh." I look down at my wristwatch, miming that I had forgotten the concept of time. "Shoot."

"Hey, you're that artist, aren't you?" The waiter opens the door an inch wider, like a turtle coming out of its shell. "Yes, I remember you. I served you, gosh, *weeks* ago." He suddenly pales, bites down hard on the inside of his cheek. "Not that I'd remember a specific detail like that. Heh. Um . . . you're just famous, you know?"

My contact-covered eyes scan his face, reading his body language. The way he still covers the vulnerable parts of his body with the door, shielding a section of his soft stomach, his left lung. The way his one exposed foot points directly at me.

I show my teeth in what could either be construed as a warm smile or a subtle threat. "Yes. I know." I take a step toward him and note how he retracts a little into the diner. I stop. "Listen, I just need a couple muffins, and you guys have my favorite. Do you have any back there I could buy from you and just be on my way?"

The waiter sucks in his cheeks. He pouts his bottom lip, thinking. I wonder what his skin would look like if I smeared it in its own color, that purple a plump gloss on his lips.

"Okay, sure," he says, and opens the door, removing what's left of his shield. "Come in."

I enter before he can change his mind.

He retreats to the back and returns moments later with a brown paper bag. He hands it to me, says they're on the house, and I blink with confusion. But when I look inside, I see the muffins he's selected are indeed my usual order: one chocolate chip, one corn. He's watched me, but when? And from where? Through the kitchen's servery window? From a back corner behind a table? Was I that ignorant of his presence or he that furtive like a field mouse? He's memorized everything he could about me in some infatuated act of devotion and he doesn't even realize it. This fond gesture was second nature to him. The behavior of a true fan.

I chuckle.

"Is everything all right?" he asks, brow furrowed, unaware of the immense intimation he's just offered me in this thin, easily shreddable bag.

"Yes. Absolutely perfect." I glance around at the chairs on top of tables. The sleeping fluorescent lights waiting to be turned on so they can whine and flicker all day. "Are you here alone?"

He nods. "I'll be opening on the late days. Got here a few hours early to clean and start setting things up."

"I see."

He taps his foot. Stretches and curls his hands at his sides like he's grasping for something.

"So, uh . . ." he starts, then points to the paper bag. "Who's the second one for?"

I tilt my head to the side and stare at him keenly. His eyes widen and he apologizes for the intrusion. But I'm not upset; I'm baffled, curious. Zahra's involvement in my life has become big news. I've been unable to escape the local headlines—*SIGHTING: FAMED ARTIST'S NEW GIRLFRIEND*; *THE NOHO DUO*; and, now, *MYSTERIOUS BEAU*—for weeks now. Mostly because the gallery owner has not stopped shoving them in my face with glee. More press means more patrons means more money.

So why would he phrase it like that? Why wouldn't he simply ask if the second muffin was for her? There was a newspaper box with our faces all over it just a few streets down, for god's sake. Is he that endearingly unaware or simply faking ignorance for some gain?

"The second muffin is for me," I answer. "Lunch."

"Boy," he says through an awkward grin. "You really like muffins."

"Yes . . . I do." I blink. Something welling up inside of me begs to laugh at this situation. "I should get going."

"Right, of course."

He follows me as I head toward the door, diner key in hand. My brain is processing ideas, actions, outcomes at a mile per minute. I turn back around to face him. His color shifts with his nerves, that brilliant purple like a weak flame I could so easily snuff out.

"Say—" I tap my empty pockets, searching for what I know is tucked away in a hidden compartment in my shirt. "Shit, I forgot my phone. But listen, I'm looking to do a new series on silhouettes. I think you'd be a great subject. Would you perhaps like my phone number and maybe we could get together under different circumstances to discuss it?"

My hand is already outstretched toward him, fingers open wide to receive what I know he will provide. At my offer, his eyes enlarge to a degree greater than I previously thought possible, and he mimics me, tapping his uniform to search for his phone. What he ends up handing me is a flip phone. Something that must be at least a decade old by now. Something without a GPS, impossible to track.

He chuckles uncomfortably. "Sorry. My income doesn't allow for much luxury. And, um—" He clears his throat. "Well, it works the same as any other phone. Messaging-wise, I mean."

"No need to apologize."

My thumbs dial in my number, hit SAVE CONTACT under *Mark Moretti*. Let him think I'll divulge a secret. My true identity, just for him.

"I look forward to hearing from you," I say.

And he looks so grateful. So devout.

On the way back to my studio, to Zahra, I tell myself it's nothing serious. Just a game I like to play.

A god with his ants.

~

Finally, the gallery is ready. My installation the owner has titled,

The Red. The unveiling will be a decadent gala. A two-day exposé during which I will be in attendance and where my work will be seen by the public eye for the first time. Normally I could care less what the petty critics think. The average Joes who believe their opinions to be worth more than their weight in gold. But I can't help but wonder . . .

I can't help but wonder what the sight of it will do to them.

Zahra stands behind the kitchen counter, palms on the cold marble, color pulsing. Her eyes are like knives positioned to cut right through me.

"What do you mean I can't come?" she asks.

I'm fiddling with my cufflinks. Smoothing and resmoothing the wrinkles in my button-down that are not wrinkles but sections where my body bends. Places I cannot permanently smooth out.

"Well," I say. "It's not a couple's event."

"It's my blood."

"It's my work."

"But that—"

"It's my profession."

"I know, but—"

"It's my life."

"Void, you're not—"

I slam my fist into the counter. "I can't be distracted!"

Zahra bites her lip. Straightens her spine and sighs.

"All right, fine," she relents. *"Fine."*

"You can come to day two. But not today. Not day one."

She nods, but the air doesn't depressurize. If anything, it's grown thick, difficult to breathe.

I ask, "Are you going to stick around or . . . ?"

"I'll grab my things and leave soon." Her fingers dig into her palms. "Have a nice night."

She disappears into my bedroom. Even without her in front of me I feel claustrophobic. Like I'm in a strong magnetic field. Like I might once again lose all sense of the meaning *personal space*. I should say goodbye. I should hug her and kiss her and explain that I just need some time alone. But what's the point of the exercise if I don't force the distance between us?

I walk out the door. Head toward the gallery. I contemplate the sky, the sorbet rainbow leading into the night. The moon that will peek through the haze until its silver glow is unignorable. All the colors I have neglected. All the light I have been so blinded to as of late.

Until now.

I place my hands on the gallery door and push. When I step inside and take in the sight, I feel like an absolute fucking rockstar. A king. A *god*.

The gallery is packed. It reeks of iron and expensive perfumes, but it's packed and it's beautiful. Immediately upon noticing me, an attendant calls for the gallery owner, who sweeps me away from the front door in an instant. She's in a shimmery gold dress and red lipstick, every inch of her dripping with unattainable wealth.

"Good evening, patrons of this fine gallery," she announces with resonance.

She was a theater kid, I think to myself. *Someone who knows how to speak from their diaphragm. Who knows how to be heard.*

She goes on to list the rules for the evening. Who can and cannot address me, what can and cannot be touched, photographed, signed. What will happen if anyone disrespects these rules, complete with a not-so-subtle gesture to the ring of black-tie bodyguards at her command.

But I'm not really paying attention to her. I'm paying attention to my art. What they've done with it.

My paintings hang along the walls out of order so that they read *resurrection, death, life, birth*. The walls are stained with the drip as though they too bleed. The drip flows into channels on the floor structured from six-inch white planks that create zigzagging patterns around the perimeter of the space. Every ten minutes, an attendant approaches with two cups to fill and then empty down the drain so that the drip may continue without overflowing.

What a ghastly scene this must be to all. Where I see Zahra's color, they—these hungry sharks circulating in and out of their pack—*they* see blood. Buckets and buckets of blood. The scent of death and metal. But they love it. They can't get enough of it. They stand before my paintings, tongues lolling from their mouths to taste the air, to taste what fraction of ichor lands amongst them. They taste for a moment too long, then wobble on weak knees to a standing table, where they have a drink to recuperate.

I hear someone vomit. When I turn to look, I find an older woman in a classic Chanel suit curled over a garbage can next to the bar. She spits up what's left in her mouth, dabs the corners of her lips with a silk handkerchief, and laughs. Laughs like she's forty years younger.

"It's been happening all night," the gallery owner whispers to me. "We've had to replace seven bins. This'll be the eighth."

I watch the older woman return to one of my paintings, Zahra's blood a glow against her wrinkled skin swallowing her up in its aura. I watch her clutch the handkerchief between her hands until her knuckles go purple. I watch how her eyes sparkle and her smile never wavers.

~

Eight drinks later and I'm as giddy as a clown. I could watch these sharks feed all night. Admire the cycle as they approach a painting, sniff at it from every corner, down another glass of mid-tier champagne, and faint into the arms of a friend, euphoric glee spread across their faces. I could watch those smiles, filled with all those sharp teeth, curl and then curl some more before the hunger takes over and they go in for another bite. Let them. Let them dine. Come one, come all, feast on the incredible Void! Have your fill of the world's greatest artist!

A voice interrupts my reverie. A shark with an inebriated grin who's strayed too far from the pack.

"Spill. Is it really your blood?"

I open my mouth to respond, but the gallery owner's voice comes out instead.

"It's art. It's subjective. It is what you believe."

"How is the drip effect possible? Does it drip from the

painting, or is it an illusion? Something behind the frame?"

"That's confidential."

The shark turns to the gallery owner, eyes wide, realizing he will not be getting an answer from me. His astonished face cracks. He smirks. He laughs. He laughs so hard his head is thrown back. His arm shoots forward and he pats me on the shoulder like I've just told a hilarious joke.

I giggle a little.

Another shark approaches, having seen the first succeed.

"So, where's the girl of the hour?" this shark asks.

A quiet hiccup leaps from my throat before I throw back a "What?"

"The girl! Zahra! We're all curious about her involvement. You know what they say, behind every great man—"

My smile fades. My blood runs cold. His words are like knives digging into my skin, unhappy with just a simple cut.

"—is a great woman. You're one lucky man, aren't you!"

"She—I'm not sure I—"

I stammer for an answer, but the gallery owner cuts in, seemingly unaware I've tried to speak for myself at all.

"Oh, yes! That darling dear. Such a beauty. Where is she, Void? I haven't seen her since . . . well, since I first met her, now that I think about it."

My fingers tremble around my glass. I lift the thin rim to my lips and sip. Tilt the glass higher and gulp. Gulp, gulp, gulp, despite all the bubbles, all the little fishies swimming down my gullet begging to get away from the sharks.

No. This isn't my story. This isn't my fated legacy.

"If you'll excuse me for just one moment."

I leave the gallery owner and the baffled sharks. I head toward the bathroom, lock the door behind me, and scream into the sink. I don't care if they hear. The gallery owner will make up some excuse.

Oh, you know. Tortured artist and all that.

I look into the mirror and see a nothing man. That colorless face. The reflective, bald head. Eyes twisted out of place because I'm drunk and my contacts have slipped down my corneas slightly. I see nothing, but it's me. Void, that empty space.

I am not Jackson Pollock. I am not encompassed by the event horizon that is my partner. The questionable shadow of a wife's influence hanging over the laborious work of artistic genius. That is *not* my story.

You know what they say. Behind every great man—

No. Behind every great man is his pain and sorrow. His experience, his past lives. There is no one else driving this machine. Only me.

My phone vibrates. I pull it from my pocket and wipe away the sweat that drips off my forehead onto the screen.

The drip ... the drip, the drip, the drip the drip thedripthedripthedripthe—

Hey, Mark! This is David.

You know, from the diner?

You probably already knew that. Haha, sorry!

Anyway, I just wanted to send you a text so you have my

number. :)

The corners of my lips curl, pull, and tighten into a smile. A shark's smile, filled with, oh, so many knives. My thumbs type slowly, calculatedly.

Hey, David! I was just thinking about you. This might seem a little forward, but are you free right now?

Oh, wow, he replies. *Yes! I am! Where would you like to meet?*

~

Everything is a haze. Me leaving the gallery, ignoring the owner's shouts and demands as she tries to catch up to me to no avail. Finding the waiter in front of my building. Hearing him say he just got off work, so he was already close by.

Taking him upstairs.

Opening the door for him. Letting him into my studio. Watching his purple color lighten and then darken, turn into shades of pink then embarrassment then back to purple again.

"Are you celebrating something?" he asks, but I don't hear him. Not really.

"Feel free to look around," I say. "Everything here is a masterpiece."

I walk to a shelf. Grab the palette knife with the lime green glow. Dangle it in the air in front of him, holding back a laugh. He looks confused, intrigued, and a little scared. He takes a step back from me.

"I carved this myself, you know," I say.

"That's very impressive."

"Me. *I* carved it. Do you understand?"

"Totally. It's very—"

It's in his throat. It splits his Adam's apple in two, then catches on his collarbone. Glorious purple comes spraying out at me, drenching my face, spilling into my open mouth, and I swallow it down. Breathe him in. Pounce like a starved animal so that his ribcage cracks beneath me when we both land on the floor. I claw my fingers into him. Tear open his skin. Yank the knife out. Ram it into his eyes. Scream into his face. Suck the juices from the blade then suck whatever scrambled mess of purple rests in his eye sockets.

He's since stopped screaming. But his body is still so warm. So *fucking* warm.

I lift the palette knife and ram it into his lower abdomen. Pull it out and stab him again and again and again, until he's a canvas of purple wounds. Torn and shredded and carved and painted.

I sit up and inhale deeply, my nostrils flaring. Wipe his blood all over my face and down my neck. Lick the flesh out from beneath my fingernails.

This is mine. This is my story. *My* design, *my* making, *my*—

A soft voice. "Void?"

I open my eyes and look up.

I see.

I see it all so clearly now.

Zahra stands before me, hands covering her mouth, tears unraveling in ribbons down her cheeks, her color growing until it

152

reaches the ceiling of my studio apartment. Behind her, through the fog of her pigment, I see the *CONGRATULATIONS!* banner. The large cake on the table riddled with candles as though it were somebody's birthday. She is dressed in lingerie, fishnet stockings up to her mid-thighs.

"Zahra?" I say with heavy breath.

I can see it in her eyes. Her reaching so high, heights no one would dare imagine. Fearless. Grasping for the sun. Only to realize she will always be destined to fall. No matter how far she climbs, the ground will always be there waiting to welcome her back into its ruinous arms.

She lets out a quiet yelp, a plea of pain from her lungs. She grabs her coat, her keys, her purse from off the kitchen counter. She runs away from me. Rushes out of my sight.

I stare at my studio. The empty canvases. The dried-up paints.

The door opens.

It shuts not with a whimper, but with a bang.

~

The gallery owner calls me at seven in the morning, and I listen to the ringtone in bed as it fills my quiet studio. The phone stops ringing and then rings again after what must be mere seconds of silence. I answer.

"Void, your paintings sold," the gallery owner says, and her ecstatic voice sounds like a cluster of tiny needles stabbing at my eardrum. "All of them. Every single *fucking* one. On opening night! Can you believe it?"

She is laughing light, fluttery laughter, and I am trying to steady my breathing.

"Void? Void, can you hear me? Did you hear what I just fucking said? Can you—"

I hang up. I return the phone to my nightstand. I turn over to lie on my back and stare at my ceiling.

Sold?

My chest hitches and I swallow like I can swallow my emotions to steady my heart.

If they've sold, that means when the exhibition is over they'll be gone. *She'll* be gone. Off to another owner, another home. She will belong to someone else, and I might never see her again.

Suddenly my bed feels cold, far too cold to lie in. I shoot up out of it and tense my calves, bounce my heels against the floor to warm my shivering body. It doesn't work. I'm freezing, my throat constricting from the chill. I exit my bedroom, my thoughts a blizzard, and upon entering the kitchen, I call out for her.

"Zahra?"

Involuntary. My body has developed the involuntary reaction to plead for her, and only now when she is not here to answer do I realize how grave her presence had become for my psyche. How necessary.

I can't help but search for her like she might be standing there in front of the stove, pan in hand, ready to make breakfast. Like I might tell her of my dilemma, as though I could explain the paradox of her needing to be here for me to express my sorrow, but that by her being here, this pain would not exist in the first place.

No. The kitchen is indeed empty, my studio quiet and vast. Because I let her get away. I let her leave without a word, not even bothering to give chase, an arrogant serpent resigned to its lonely nest. And when I turn to the vinyl tarps, only then do I remember that I am not alone. The waiter is here with me.

I approach the dead body in its pool of purple and kneel beside it to inspect the damage. The waiter's front is a massacre of gashes and tears. His lips have been slathered in his own color, plump and still vibrant beneath the pigment. I could imagine him sitting upright, rising from the floor to smile at me, if not for the fact that his eyes are gone, pockets of gore in their place. I peer into them and witness a shimmer of color. He looks beautiful. I can understand that he looks beautiful as a concept, the purple ornate polka dots decorating his being, but I can't feel it. I am numb.

I brush a clump of hair out of his face and wonder if this would make him Number Twelve. If he would be considered an addition to my palette. The thought feels vile. Not just untrue, but blasphemous. I want to call out for Zahra again, to apologize for ever thinking such a thought, but I bite my tongue.

She is not here.

She is gone.

And this is what I have chosen over her. Someone who could never understand my art. Someone who cannot withstand my existence. Someone who is dead and who bleeds in one dimension.

~

I am standing in line for the Ferris wheel amongst the colors, as though I am one of them. Like I could ever understand what it means to have a hue. The wheel rotates, high and mighty in the sky. The spokes, the wires, the metal. The snails curling and uncurling, an infinite spiral.

I ignore my phone vibrating in my pocket. The gallery owner texting and calling, wanting to be assured I will make it tonight.

After what must be the fiftieth buzz, I pull out my phone and fire back one text.

I'll be there.

"Ticket?"

A hand extends into my line of sight, blocking my phone screen.

I lift my head and face a man dressed in a red-and-orange-striped muscle tee with eggplant harem pants. He has a green beret on, and I don't know how to tell him that, along with the bright yellow cloud surrounding him, he is a walking mess. His colors clash. His colors will never work together no matter how hard he might try.

Instead, I hand him my ticket, a little piece of paper like what you might rip off a raffle wheel.

"Take the next seat," he says.

I pass the metal gate, which he shuts behind me. I approach the wheel. It goes around and around and around. A giant spiral. The Ferris wheel car slows to a stop at the platform where another man, this one in a similarly offending get-up highlighting blues and pinks, gestures for me to enter through open doors. I take my seat. The metal is cold beneath me. I place my palms on either side of my thighs, feel that chill up my wrists and forearms.

The Ferris wheel jolts to a start. My car sways forward then back, then settles as it climbs. I take a moment to acknowledge the ride, then glance above and below at the changing colors in other cars.

Anticipation. Excitement. Lust. Fear. Relief. One color strobes, then turns red, then turns into forgiveness. One color is trying its hardest to remain happy.

All these colors, they clash. They're all too much all the time, aren't they? It's a palette of excess. That's all it is. They just muddle each other up.

The snails should come. They should come and nibble away. They should consume and consume this extra light. These spectrums that no one really cares for.

That'll show them. That'll show them what's important.

I don't even realize I'm at the top until the wheel jolts to a stop and my car swings me back into the present.

The top. The tippy-top, where the snails can't reach me. If I turn to the sky, I see only the blue expanse and the sun. I stare at the sun, eyes wide, feeling the rays pierce the soft jelly of my corneas. There is no pleasure. It hurts, like my eyes are swelling and bleeding all at once inside my skull. When the pain is too much I turn away with a quiet shout, tears spilling. I blink. I stare at the streets below. At the tiny samples of color moving about like ants. Like microscopic bugs the snails will surely eat.

I search for one color in particular.

I search for her amongst the excess.

~

Day two of the gallery opening feels more like torture than delight. Like a sick exploitation of my suffering. I can't stand this audience, these wealthy patrons with lipstick-stained teeth and jaundiced skin the gallery owner ushers me to and from. I ask her for a drink, and then another drink, and hope that the next one will stop me from grinding my teeth. Stop the tension headache from shooting up into my temples. Stop me from searching for Zahra standing there expectantly in her green dress in the empty spaces of this gallery.

This room makes me sick. All these colors blending over Zahra's is an abomination. Frankly, no one should be here right now. No one should be laying their eyes upon her.

Someone pulls me away from staring out the gallery windows, searching. They have some asinine question for me, a question like all the other questions, and I want to snarl. Bare my teeth and snap at them like a rabid dog.

I don't get the chance.

The gallery doors burst open. There's a commotion. A rustling in the crowd. I'm approached by two men in gray suits balancing some video equipment. A microphone is shoved in my face, and I must stop myself in my rabid state from chomping down on it, breaking my teeth against the metal.

"Mr. Void, was it a stunt?" one asks.

"Is it all a part of this exhibition?" asks the other.

"Is she really dead?"

Is she really dead . . . ?

I open my mouth, eyebrows strained toward each other. My head tilts. Questions. All these fucking questions, but I can't make sense of them now.

Is she really dead . . . ?

The gallery owner steps in front of me like a shield, hands raised to deflect what I am now realizing are a couple of tabloid reporters.

"What the hell is going on here?" she hisses. "This is a closed event. I specifically requested no media presence."

"We're not here for the event."

"Well, not directly."

The man with the microphone, the leader with the rose hue and distant eyes, turns back to me. "Mr. Void. Are you aware that at 9:38 this morning, Zahra Saeed jumped in front of a subway car on the Upper East Side?"

Is she really—?

I don't think I process it at first. I think the words just spill out of his mouth, and internally I am laughing at this man who thinks he can make any sense to me. Who thinks he has the right questions. The questions that will reveal insights far beyond his comprehension. No. Not these kindergarten-grade queries.

What paint did you use?

What's your favorite medium? Your favorite painting?

Is it true it's all Zahra's blood?

"Mr. Void?"

A hand grabs my wrist. Long nails dig into my skin.

"My god," the gallery owner whispers.

Why are you so amazed by these two? I want to ask her. *They're nothing but fools.*

"You must be joking," she says.

"I'm afraid not, ma'am."

The gallery owner turns to me, and I'm searching her eyes for confirmation. For my truth—

They're children, don't you get it? They don't know the right questions to ask.

—but her eyes don't agree. They see a different truth.

"Now that you mention it, a girl did burst in here at around nine a.m.," the gallery owner says to the reporters. "I was walking the floor when she marched in, and I thought it was just some homeless person from the street. She looked awful. Her hair was completely disheveled, matted like a nest, and her clothing and hands were terribly dirty, like she'd slept all night on the street. I couldn't get a good look at her since the sun was in my eyes, but she kept turning away from me to look at the paintings. She was frantic—very, *very* frantic, taking in each frame—and her body was so stiff. I told her to leave, but she wouldn't listen. Eventually she just screamed. It was so shrill, so very awful. I had to cover my ears. And then she ran out the door." The gallery owner sees me again, her eyes dilating with pity. "I suppose that could have been Zahra?"

There's a pause. One that prickles my skin, sinks its fangs into my throat so that I am too choked up to speak.

The snails. I'm afraid they've all dried up under the sun.

"Do you take me for an idiot?"

We both turn to the reporter. His red face matches his now enraged color.

"Zahra Saeed, suddenly *homeless*?" he says. "What kind of a cheap story is that? I had my fucking doubts and I knew it. This is all for the exhibition, isn't it? Her body wasn't even found, did you know that? Allegedly only pieces of her. Minced meat. All we have are eyewitness accounts, and that's shit. Those could be faked by anyone. This stunt is as cheap as that story. I'm not reporting propaganda and getting laughed at. Next time you want advertising, pay for it like everyone else."

The reporters storm out. The gallery is left in silence. I look around at all those faces, all those lonely, concerned faces staring back at me, and only now do I realize.

The paintings.

Her color.

The drip has stopped.

It's all stains now.

It's all dried-up stains.

MONA KABBANI

ACHROMATIC

MONA KABBANI

I have ridden the Ferris wheel thirty-two times now, one ticket for every day since, five revolutions each, one hundred and sixty rotations around the sun.

I am on rotation number one hundred and sixty-one.

I need to ride the Ferris wheel. I need to reach the sun. I think one day maybe I'll reach it. Or I'll find her. Or I'll break my body against the earth and never heal. One will come first. One will come, eventually. One must. But I feel her absence. Not just from my life, but from this world. The spectrums seem a little darker, stripped of that shifting, oil-slick hue.

So I ride. I ride and I ride, no longer feeling like a god, or even an active participant in this universe, but a nothing that has somehow managed to lose everything.

~

The gallery owner has renewed my contract. The shareholders demanded it, and she is not one to argue with the money. They'll lower their commission, funnel a large portion of the marketing budget in my favor, dedicate a wall to my name amongst other pot sweeteners in exchange for my time. Ten years' exclusivity instead of three.

I tell her it might as well be a life sentence for all I care and sign it before she puts together the missed opportunity: the additional years, whatever remains of my life, signed and sealed in her pocket like the beads of an abacus.

But in the end, she'll still get a decade.

She locks the contract away in her desk with a reptilian smile and says it's a pleasure doing business with me. And before I leave, she tells me to keep up the eccentricities.

"Your strange behavior has been good for the gallery. It attracts the patrons."

It's been over a month. A month and three days since Zahra. Every day I think I see her on the street, in a café, around the corner, only to find it's some other dark-haired woman with a color not worth noting. For a month and three days, I have sent text message after text message to her cell phone, praying for a response, for the fiber-optic ether to speak back.

Zahra.

Zahra, are you there?

Were you ever really there?

Please. I need you.

For a month and three days, I have waited for the cops to knock on my door. I have waited for them to tell me they have found her body, matched the color of her blood to my paintings, and will be taking me in for questioning, willingly or in handcuffs.

But they never do.

So every day I wait, and every day I clean. I clean because I do not, in my current state of mind, have the will to paint. I am paranoid and self-destructive and unguided. I clean my studio like it's an affront to all those questions I do not wish to answer. Is she dead? Was she ever even here? Those kindergarteners know now. They know what to ask. And if only they'd *fucking shut up so I could keep my head together long enough to form a coherent thought.* But I have tabloid headlines to prove it. The art installation itself, for god's sake! She was here. I *know* she was. Yet the installation has dried up and shriveled away like a delineation on the stages of decay, and I can't even see it anymore. Each piece is in its new home, removed from me, gone from my sight forever. Newspapers age and headlines fade, and I'm worried I'll start to forget. I'll start to doubt. Maybe I already have. I have erased her from my floorboards. I have done exactly what I swore to never do—the obliteration of *us*, the proof our infatuation existed in the first place—and in doing so I have erased myself. Where does one go from here? Surely not up. At least not high enough. Eventually I'll fall, if I haven't yet already, unable to see where I slipped and where I'll crash so that I have fooled myself into believing I am still on stable ground. So I clean. I clean away. I clean the studio every night before I sleep because if she no longer gets to exist there, nothing does.

That reminds me, I've run out of bleach. I wonder what an installation painted with nothing but bleach would look like. What would the gallery owner say if I presented her with eleven blank canvases and told her all the warped threads were from bleach, a product whose raison d'être is the removal of color? Would she find it cataclysmic? Would she scream at me until her head loosed from her neck like a burst balloon?

In the store, I know exactly where to find the bleach. The grocery clerks do not ask me if I need help, knowing I'll leave with the same singular item I have left with once every week for the past five weeks. The cashier takes my money and looks at me for a second too long. He bags my bleach and passes it over, his lips pressed into a tight line. I thank him, no longer needing to tell him to keep the change, always feeling strange about using the money made from Zahra's blood.

Along the walk back to my studio, I watch the passing cars with their dull paint jobs drive down the road. It's a mildly warm, breezy day, and I like how all their windows are rolled down, arms clouded with whatever colors I could not be bothered to analyze resting against their aluminum doors. I watch one car, tan and falling apart around its axles, race down this thin city street at what must be fifty miles per hour. As if my sight, my very destructive thoughts, triggered it, the car screeches to a halt, causing a domino effect of tire burns and angry shouts. One car notices too late and swerves to avoid a collision, its front right tire jumping the curb onto the sidewalk. A nearby pedestrian screams like she's just witnessed an atrocity. The driver tells her to shut it.

There's a commotion, an orchestra of rage, fumes of gasoline and burnt rubber, and, from above it all, a laugh. It's carefree and light, like a soft feather riding the heatwaves of a forest fire. It comes from someone who knows they are invincible even in the face of a speeding vehicle. Even in the face of imminent death.

I know that laugh.

I look to that first car and see the outline of something, of some*one*, the silhouette of a girl emerging from the front bumper. She laughs and she twirls, her hair creating a skirt around her face as the people of this city shout at her. Demand that she watch where she's going next time. Ask her how she could be such a fucking moron.

But she doesn't hear—or chooses not to—as she skips onto the sidewalk and disappears between two buildings.

Drivers get back into their vehicles and carry on, just another day in the city, and I am left with a bag of bleach and a quivering bottom lip. I take one step forward, then another, my heart threatening to shoot up into my throat, butterflies in my chest with their fiberglass wings I have not felt for so very long.

God, when was the last time I felt this feeling so violently?

I reach the corner and peer inside.

I see her back. I see her watching the sun on its journey to meet the horizon.

I see her waiting for me.

"Zahra?"

She turns around, and the sight of her ruptures every system in my body. Her chin, her neck, her very stance that declares her place in this world. But her face. Her face is a topography of canyons and curves: furrowed brow; downturned lips; drooping, sunken eyes. She looks so . . . lost.

"Zahra." I step forward. I'm in tears. "My god, *Zahra*—"

Are you happy? I want her to ask. I want her to ask like she always did in those fleeting moments I thought unimportant and the answer obvious. But she doesn't seem to understand what I need, what we *both* need, and that's okay. I can do it for her. I should have done it from the start.

"Zahra, I'm so happy to see you," I breathe.

She takes a hesitant step away from me. Her head tilts to the side.

And in her voice—that voice I have felt shatter against my skin in cosmic waves for nights on end—she asks, "I'm sorry, do I know you?"

My expression falls. My nerves have cooled as though a glacier swept through my veins, and I am trembling.

"Of . . . of course you know me. Zahra. Zahra, it's me."

She's shaking her head.

"I'm not Zahra."

"Not Zahra?"

And now I too am shaking my head, and we are both shaking our heads like we've caught ourselves in a nest of gnats, and I am lamenting and pleading and begging her to stop it. To please just *stop it* and understand.

I have died every day since without you.

"I know you, Zahra," I press. "I'd know you were the world consumed by eternal night and your soul a pocket of darkness. I would recognize you by your laugh, your smell, the way you breathe, and even if I'd lost all sense of sight I'd know you by the rhythm your footsteps make to accompany the music your existence creates in my head. I know you and I have loved you not by the absence of your flaws but by the presence of your darkness. How you dig your nails into your palms to break your skin when you're worried or stressed, how you can only feel joy in the forced moments of blissful pain. I know you like paint knows a canvas, like the waves know the shore. I know you like my wounds know heat and the sun knows the sky, and I especially know you by your color—"

I drop the bleach. It hits the asphalt and the plastic container cracks open. Noxious liquid oozes from the bag and creates a puddle near the rubber sole of my right foot.

The sun, in joining us between these two city buildings, has hit just right, and I didn't think to look at her color, to see her as a composite to be scrutinized in bits and pieces as I once did rather than simply Zahra, the girl I fell in love with, to see what has become of it until now.

Her color is black. Achromatic, like tar, like soot, like the endless expanse of space where light is long, long dead. I stare at it, unable to speak, my mouth opening and closing like a fish overwhelmed with the vastness of the deep, and it stares back. The color at the end of everything.

Emerging from this infinitely dimensional space—for surely there are pockets within pockets, increments that hold their own infinities—are spirals. Spirals that start small then grow with every rotation. Hundreds of them, thousands, and I watch them, transfixed, until mentally I am swearing to the god I once thought I occupied that my own eyes are not pupils, not the empty holes where light enters and is processed, but spirals. Pools and pools of spirals.

Zahra is speaking. She is saying things I cannot understand because it is not only color that I am seeing but shapes for the first time in my pretentious life, and I am hypnotized, and if she asked me, I would carve that shape, that spiral with its loops and loops, never finding its own end, always finding more and more space to expand into, across my body. To show her that I would never want to heal from this.

"Void!"

"What?" I whisper, and I realize I don't know if she's addressing me or the portal around her she surely can sense.

She clears her throat, readjusts her stance like a girl preparing to ask a boy to the prom. Her fingers dig into each other, and I pray she'll bleed. I pray to see if the Stygian, spiraling effects outside have taken ahold within.

"Things have changed," she tells me. "I am not Zahra. At least, I'm not *your* Zahra. Not anymore."

She does not bleed. She does not dig her nails in too hard and pop her skin open like lava from the core of the earth. She does not drip, drip, drip onto the floor and show the shadows and asphalt they know nothing of darkness.

She turns. She walks away from me. She walks, unscathed, out of the alley and toward the setting sun.

~

What possessed Jackson Pollock to employ the drip technique? Of all the styles of art, the methods and forms, in the end the drip is what called to him. Was it the way he could become the brush, the palette, the knife? The way his very movement created images—chaotic strokes that at first glance seem to be without guidance, without meaning, yet revolutionized abstract expressionism. Those same chaotic strokes viewers would ponder for hours until the weight of their eyelids forced them to turn away. Did his senescence drive him mad when he realized his body could no longer function as the apparatus it once did? Did he come to the awful conclusion that, despite his success, success that made him impervious to all but himself, none of it had nor ever would fulfill him? Not truly. He couldn't pick up what he had created, accomplished, seen—each experience like a polished coin—and hold them in his weak, thinning fingers to find comfort. No one would be there to help keep his trembling arms in the air for long enough, or to keep the coins from slipping between his bones so he could gaze at these mementos forever. These coins, although brilliant on the outside, were hollow in the end, and he felt the lack of their weight with crushing despair on the nights he found himself alone. Not alone for a lack of admiration, the physical presence of bodies about him, but truly, utterly alone.

Yet for all his experiments, his leaps of faith, the one part of the artistic process he never undertook was to *be* the paint. To see not only what his limbs could do but what his insides could be. And as I kneel here atop the vinyl tarps in my studio, thighs pressed against the edge of a blank canvas, palette knife in hand, blade inert, indenting my bare stomach, I can't help but wonder if the secret to absolution rests deep within. If all it takes is a short swipe—the same movement I have done to many others before— to reveal the truth. Maybe if I dig in deep enough, bleed for long enough, I'll see. I'll see what color sits inside of me. I'll see it and it will be something extraordinary and I'll show it to Zahra and say, *Now you have proof that we are each one of a kind. We are made for each other. I made this for you and you are mine.* And then, because the blood is rushing out of me faster than I can reproduce it, and because I cannot sew myself together with an invisible thread, I'll die in her arms. My final masterpiece, a last act, a declaration of love, a dedication to her.

But it's a matter of finding that color first. Of pulling it out of me no matter the cost. Am I willing to do it? Willing to go so far? Such a sacrifice in the name of a greater pursuit. Think through this. It could be anywhere—not necessarily in the center of my core, but anywhere at all. My heart, my calf, my liver.

My eyes.

I can see it now. Digging the knife into my socket, pulling out the soft jelly, the very organ that has allowed me to see the spectrums I do, harboring the one color I have long desired. I can see myself staring at myself in a very real, paradoxical way, an emotion like anger swelling up inside of me from finally discovering my color behind that barren pupil—anger, but also relief, all bottled up inside until I can take it no longer and the physical manifestation of these uncontainable emotions results in squeezing my eye like a putty, like a clay, until it pops between my fingers.

I'll take that viscera, that pigment that is something other than crimson, and swipe at my canvas. Fingerpaint with heated delirium until I realize I am outlining the image of Zahra's face.

I raise the blade, angle it in a downward motion just above my head, feel my pupils dilate on the glinting, sharp end. I wonder if I could somehow paint Zahra's color with my own, an alchemy of sorts. A transmutation of light. A seduction toward something so dark, something with shapes and spirals and who knows what else that might lurk within. I wonder if I could turn myself into a part of her.

Unlike that reporter, I believe Zahra jumped. I believe she stood on the edge of the subway platform, distraught, suffering. I believe she stared into the tracks, licked her lips at how inviting the abyss beneath them looked, how dark and cold and endless. I believe she thought she could bury herself so deep the sun would never find her.

She jumped—or better yet, she fell.

And she fell.

And she fell.

And she fell.

Until the ground turned into the sky and she landed, *finally* landed back on her feet. Then, from the torn flesh, the broken bones, the shattered ligaments, she rose.

Is she dead?

Was she ever really here?

I know the answers now. I could take the stairs to my rooftop and shout from the depths of my lungs. She has been here far longer than any of us, but I am the only one to see. How she resurrects. How she becomes more with every death, something imminent, something that smothers each precedent of greatness she set in her previous life until she is anew.

I think about lying with her on these very tarps, holding her in my arms, and inhaling her scent. Would she smell any different now that I know? Would I be able to distinguish the degree of metamorphosis between every one of her rebirths, her scent flavored with an extra drop of charcoal each time? And her eyes— I wasn't close enough in the alleyway to see, but were her eyes different? No longer oil-slick, but black, and drowning in spirals? If we were to go to dinner, would all gaze upon her beauty but none see the horrors I see? The terrific, dark delights I witness day after day?

What properties will she emerge with upon her next death? Upon the one after that, and the one after that, and the one after—

Falling, falling, always falling.

I remove the knife from my line of sight, flex, and drag the blade down my bicep, splitting open the skin. When the blood finally pools, I dip my fingers into the red and lean over the canvas, not caring that a part of me is dripping—*drip, drip, dripping*—directly onto it. Not caring that the design won't be perfect.

I press my fingers into the white, draw a small circle, miss the connection, then draw a larger circle, all-encompassing to compensate; miss, compensate, miss, compensate, miss, compensate. I do this over and over and over again, not stopping until I am faint and the sun's rays are dripping into my studio and the canvas is nothing but a red square. I smile, knowing what's within the folds of all that red—*the spirals*—and fall onto my back. Staring up at my ceiling, I'm laughing now, inspired to paint, inspired to fall. To paint and fall and paint *and fall and paint and—*

One day I will create my final masterpiece and it will belong to Zahra. One day I will behold my color, and Zahra will be the only one alive to know of its pigment. One day I will die, and it will be Zahra wondering if I was ever with her in the first place.

But not today. Not anytime soon.

There is too much to discover, to witness, to create. Too much to touch, to taste, to smell. Things I have been placed here to endure, to document, to experience. I will find Zahra. I will hold her tight and make it clear that I will never let go. Even when she falls, we will fall together. That is what the universe demands, the sun purrs, the snails whisper:

She is owed to me.

MONA KABBANI

AFTERWORD

In college, I made a bracelet and carved the symbol for arsenic into its wooden beads. I gave this bracelet as a gift to a boy I was in a two-year-long tumultuous relationship with. I thought it was love. I somehow thought that if I recognized our relationship for what it was—*toxic*—declared it, and made some kind of symbolic testament to my willingness to persevere despite all the pain, I was defining love.

He took the bracelet, thanked me in a multitude of ways, then showed it to his friends and laughed.

True story.

I realized years later after damagingly romantic thoughts of him ceased to cross my mind, how tragic that was. How deluded I had allowed myself to become in the pursuit of love.

Love is not difficult. It should not hurt. But like alcohol, when you drink the right amount of poison, it can feel deceivingly good.

When the concept of spectrally bound lovers first came to mind, I had intended a different, less homicidal plot. Yet still after the many treatments leading to what is now *The Color of Blood*, the beats have always remained the same: two people fall madly in love, their egos get in the way, they fall traumatically out of love, they get back together only for the cycle to perpetuate.

Four years ago when this concept first lingered in my head as a small, translucent bead, I had wanted to call the story *Happy* as a testament to what toxic relationships steal from those involved. I thought about that old title as I wrote this book, reflecting on my own experiences, imbuing my grievances into these characters. Zahra's persistent question—*"Are you happy?"*—is one I ask of myself and of others daily. I think it's important.

Now, I have many people to thank, all of whom make me immeasurably happy, so let's begin.

ACKNOWLEDGMENTS

First, I would like to make clear that although the world of art is a fascinating one, it is not one I am intimately familiar with. Any inaccuracies regarding art-related topics are the cursory effects of Void's chaotic state of mind and not the mistakes of the beautiful souls who aided this work.

To Kristopher Triana. Thank you for your guidance over the course of this project. This story would not be the same without you. I'm honored to call you my mentor and my friend.

To Spencer Hamilton. Mama, can you believe we are already on book number four? I'm so thankful to have you by my side. Here's to many more projects to come!

To my loving parents. When I told them the plot of this story, they gave me a thumbs-up, albeit a trembling one. Thank you for your constant love and support.

To my partner, Jack Mihalcik. Baby, there ain't a toxic thing about you. Thank you for being the greatest partner and filling my every day with the most vibrant hue of love.

An extended thanks goes to all my family and loved ones: Lauren Downey for being a good friend and supporting my writing career from day one; Kyla Frasche for taking my hand and guiding me in the ways of Procreate, dealing with my tantrums while I worked and reworked the cover art to perfection; Teta Mona; Teta Mila and Jiddoh; Vilena Baranova alongside Olivia and Daniel Darensbourg; Todd Saunders; Ashley Wojtkowiak; Amy Teegan; Nouni Mouallem and Nada Kabbani; and so many more. I love you all.

And finally to you, my dear reader. This book would not be possible without you.

Mona Kabbani
February 24, 2024

Mona Kabbani is a horror fan, writer, and reviewer obsessed with psychology and the human condition. She emulates the conflict of the good versus the bad and all of the in between in her work while providing an entertainingly horrifying experience. She is the author of *The Bell Chime*, which won the award for Best Horror Novella of 2020 from LoHF, *Vanilla*, and *For You*. She is a Lebanese immigrant living the dream in New York City where much of her writing is inspired. You can follow her on Instagram and TikTok @moralityinhorror for more and sign up for her mailing list on her website, www.moralityinhorror.com.

MONA KABBANI

Made in United States
Orlando, FL
04 January 2025

56870005R00114